WAIT ON ME

KNIGHTS OF RETRIBUTION MC #2

ELIZABETH KNOX

EST.
1979
KNIGHTS OF RETRIBUTION

CONTENTS

Here Kitty, Kitty
Booger
Widow
Kade
Hawk
Bull
Cobra
Mouser
Dixon
Zane
Amara
Grim
Chaz
Frost
Zorro
Axel
Hammer

SERIES: IRON VEX MC
Enraged
Bossed Up
Vex's Temptation
Venom's Secret

SERIES: ROYAL BASTARDS MC: BALTIMORE/KNIGHTS OF
RETRIBUTION MC
Bet on Me

Rely on Me

Hate on Me

Wait on Me

SERIES: SATAN'S RAIDERS MC

Inc's Regret

SERIES: THE CLANS WITH IRIS SWEETWATER

Promised

The Trade

Cherished

Deceit

Love is War

Defiant

Shattered

Ruthless

Covert

Heretic

Venomous

Flawed

Demise

SERIES: THE MACKENZIE & VOLKOLV DUET

Deceptive Love

SERIES: LOVE HACK

Ransom

Anthologies

Romanticizing the Gods
The Elementals

Boxsets

Claiming Their Mates: A Hells Gateway MC Boxset

Trigger Warning

This book is intended for mature audiences only. If darker books are not for you, please do not move forward. After re-adjusting my trigger warning system, I will *not* be giving any spoilers. Please understand that this is not your run-of-the-mill romance and tough subjects will be discussed in this storyline. This story could include things like rape, kidnapping, abuse, domestic violence, drugs, alcohol abuse, and *many* other potential triggers.

Please also be advised it is *not* recommended to read this book as a standalone.

RAVAGE

10 Years Ago . . .

"I can't believe we're here."

Marisole turns to look at me, an amused smirk dragging across her face. "You still didn't think we'd come, did you?"

Well, she's got me there. "I thought you were pullin' my leg when you said we were takin' a trip to Mexico. Then you said we'd be stayin' at a resort, everythin' was paid for, and I . . . Marisole, I love you, but I thought you were screwin' with me." Part of me thinks she still might be. Hell if I know, but here we are, two people in our early twenties, at a fancy-ass resort we obviously can't afford.

Marisole hasn't ever talked about her dad much. I've been dating the woman for two years and she briefly mentioned him around the holidays we've spent together. Now we're in Mexico? I try to keep my personal feelings to myself cause this seems weird as shit, but she's been excited to come down here and see her father. Who am I to take her down a few notches? It doesn't take a genius to figure out she has an abnormal relationship with her dad. Still, she must respect him if she's willing to drop everything for a visit. The fact she asked me to tag along wasn't expected, but I'm taking this as an opportunity.

There's not a doubt in my mind I'll end up meeting him at some point this weekend, and there's something I need to ask him. I didn't think about asking him prior to this trip, considerin' he's never been around, but coming here shows me how much Marisole does respect him. The mere fact she thinks highly of him means I need to change my plans.

There's been a question I've wanted to ask Marisole for a few months now and I haven't been able to find the right time. She's the light of my life and I need her to brighten up my dark days. I need her so much I don't want anyone else. We may be young, but when you know, you know.

Since we're here, I can do something I didn't think

I would. I can ask for her father's blessing and it'll make our proposal even more special to her. Not to mention we're in a beautiful place where she deserves to be proposed to. She doesn't deserve me asking for her hand in marriage while we're in Highlandtown watching women pimp themselves out on the corner.

No, she deserves something like this.

Something as beautiful as she fuckin' is.

Marisole's golden brown hair falls over her shoulders effortlessly and she releases an adorable giggle. "My father wanted me to come down, so he handled everything."

Even though she seems to be fine on the outside, plastering on a smirk and laughing, her eyes tell me a different story. I want to ask what's bothering her, but I don't. If I do, it could cause us to get into a fight because the woman doesn't like being pushed. When she wants to come out and tell me what's bothering her, she will.

The sun illuminates her hair and Marisole pulls out a compact from her purse. Flipping it open, she grabs one of her lip glosses and draws her brows together. I know exactly what she's doing. She can't make up her mind. "Babe, what looks better on my lips?" Marisole turns to me, and I stare in awe at how she can look beautiful in just about anything. Whether it's an oil-ridden t-shirt with her hair in a messy bun or in what she calls full glam.

She's wearing a white top and skirt set that matches. The skirt starts above her belly button and conforms to her natural curves, while there's a slit that starts mid-thigh on her left leg. Teal, red, purple, and yellow flowers line the top of the skirt and stop, almost lookin' like flowers that're fallin' from a vine. Meanwhile, her top has the same flowers around the bottom hem. The flowers stop just below her ample bust and she immediately starts laughing, so carefree.

"I thought you'd like this outfit, but golly, you look like you want to ravage me."

"There's a reason I got my road name, baby girl," I tease. Standing up, I stalk toward her and slide my hands over her chunky ass once I'm within reach. I snake a hand up her side and glance down at her succulent peach lips. "You ask me what I think looks better . . . how about this?" I bring my lips down onto hers, and she inhales sharply but smiles against my lips.

Even two years later, we've still got it. A lot of couples can't say that shit.

I steal this kiss from her, lingering for as long as I can, knowing we need to get going. We have dinner with her father and we can't be late.

Marisole doesn't know it yet, but tonight her life will change forever.

Tonight, she'll no longer be my girlfriend. She'll be my fiancée.

MARISOLE

Present Day...

Leaning back on the rusty muted green bench stool, I revel at sitting in this dark room. Well, it's not a room. It's a small makeshift garage that's only for my husband's use. Scar is the Prez of the Beasts of Brutality MC. Everyone here both respects him and fears him. He's terrifying and I only know a bit of the things he's done.

Massacre, one of the oldest men in the club, told me one time that Rage was shaping Scar to be his protégé. All of the men in the Beasts of Brutality MC were part of the Demons of Hell MC before they were forced into hiding. Their former Prez, who's now dead, Rage, had pissed off the wrong people. He had enemies stacked miles high, but his alliances were just as solid until they all came crumbling down.

One of his allies was my father, Rafael Ramirez. For a long time, I didn't understand why my father would align himself with a man like Rage, but I quickly understood the reasoning for his choices.

My father's empire was beginning to fall and he saw his end coming. He's been dead for years now, and Rage died three years ago. This may sound twisted, but I come from a sick family, so my thoughts aren't out of character. I only wish my father died before he further solidified his alliance with Rage. In doing so, he promised my hand in marriage to his protégé, and we've been married for almost ten years.

They've been the most grueling, exhausting years of my life. Years I thought I wouldn't ever be able to endure and somehow, I still don't know how I've been able to survive it. Scar should've killed me by now. After all, my father's dead and my protection is no longer guaranteed. But he hasn't even made an attempt on my life. Sure, he does the most fucked up things to me but never once has he crossed a line he can't come back from.

I've been handed off to his men like a clubwhore. Tied up and forced into physically painful positions while being defiled by the men in his club, doing whatever it is they want to my body. Scar lights a match and brings the flame until it burns my skin, just to get a reaction from me. He's put out his cigarettes on me, cut my hair off, has really done anything someone could imagine to defile and make me feel worthless.

I pull the string that hangs somewhere above my head and the light illuminates more of the dark garage. Looking at the tools laid out on the wood table in front of me, I pick up a wrench and skim my fingertips along the cool metal, wishing things ended up differently. My life could've been so much different.

"He's great. Isn't he?" I smile at my father, hoping he sees Ravage as the well-mannered man he is. He treats me great and I've been with him for two years at this point. Two years and he hasn't ever done anything he can't come back from. We're comfortable with each other and I love him. I just want my father to see I'm being taken care of.

My father's expression falters the second we're in his study out of Ravage's view. He shuts the door firmly and finally speaks his mind, "I want to agree with you, but he's . . . dull, mija."

Taken aback by his words, I blink a few times, trying to process what he's said. "Dull?" I repeat.

Immediately, he nods. "He's not what you need."

"What? How can you say something like that?" He

doesn't even know him. Not at all. He's spoken to him for maybe two hours.

"In our family, you become good at reading people, mija. Plus, I told you I had a plan for your future. One that involves a man of importance, not a . . . a man like him. You are of a high-born bloodline, which means I've already arranged a marriage for you. A marriage to a man of power."

There's no way he can be serious right now. I narrow my eyes at him and suck in a sharp breath. "Where is all this coming from? You've never once spoken to me about this," I grumble, walking toward the window that overlooks his garden area. Even though he lives within twenty minutes of the beach, his estate is smack dab in the middle of the desert. Forty-foot walls surround his home like they would in the movies. "Why haven't you said anything to me before? This all seems so . . . convenient, given the timing."

"I wanted to wait until you were twenty. I haven't been around as much as I'd like to have been, but this marriage, this alliance, is a gift for you. The man I've negotiated for you to marry is Rage's son, Scar."

Rage? Who is Rage? "Wait. Are you talking about the man from my quinceañera?" There were many people at my quinceañera, people I'd never met my entire life, but Rage . . . I remember the man with the dark hair, his piercing eyes, and most of all, the look that will forever be burned into my memory.

"Yes, mija. His son, Scar, is who you will marry. I've arranged for you to be married on your birthday. So until then, you are a free woman. Have fun with this . . . dull beast until then. But on your—"

"If you're about to say what I think you are—don't—I don't give a damn what you arranged. I'm not going to marry someone I've never met. As a matter of fact, you won't ever get to choose who I—" I don't see it coming at all. The sudden movement in the air should've been enough of a sign. However, it isn't. The back of my father's hand rips against my skin and it burns like if I spilled hot water on myself. Shock swarms over me and I take a few steps back. With widened eyes, I try to gauge if this is my reality or if I'm losing my mind a bit.

My father takes two long strides toward me and grimaces. "You will do what I say when I say. If it wasn't for me, you wouldn't even be here right now. Your mother never wanted to have you in the first place. I paid her to make sure she didn't abort you. Remember that the next time you try and disobey me."

Shaking my head, tears spill down my cheeks in an effortless flow. Even now, the power of his words still rings in my mind, causing me the worst amount of emotional pain. What he said to me that day is something I shouldn't have ever heard.

My life is worthless. I can't make any decisions for myself and I'm nothing but a tool, just like the wrench my fingers skirt along. My life isn't even my own and I'm tired of not having any control.

I take my hands away from the wrench and look on the wooden table, realizing there's an extension cord not being used. I take in a deep breath and am unable to tear my eyes away from the cord. My heart's pumping hard in my chest, almost like my body is begging me to stop this before it's too late, but I can't.

This is it. This is my *only* way out of this hellhole.

I unwrap the cord and look around the garage, trying to see what I can tie it to. The garage is an average metal pole building and the ceilings are high. Then again, I'm about five foot two, so everything is tall to me. I stand up on the stool, toss the cord over the metal beam a couple feet above me, and pull the opposite side down. Within a minute, I've tied a few knots into the cord, so my body weight doesn't pull it undone.

Next, I wrap the cord around my neck and toss it again over the rafter, pulling the other side of the cord down and secure it. This will work. It has to. I don't want to keep being an object to these people anymore. I don't want to keep living a life that isn't even my own. I can't, and I won't.

I take in one last breath and look down, knowing my body will hang a good foot or two. Worry courses through me. I hope this won't hurt too bad. It can't be worse than the things Scar's done to me. It just can't.

Closing my eyes, I kick the stool down so I can't back out of this shit and it hits the concrete with a loud *thud*.

My body takes over and goes into fight or flight mode and I gasp for air, desperately trying to get it. It's ironic. My body wants me to try and breathe, to fight for this shitty thing I call life, but my mind isn't amused by this joke.

The door to the garage is pushed open and three bodies come filing in. Pressure comes around my legs and then everything goes black. The darkness consumes me and I hope this is it.

I hope I never wake up to this nightmare ever again.

CHAPTER TWO

RAVAGE

The languid flames flicker in the bonfire in front of us. Things have been relaxed lately, which is a nice change of scenery from what it's typically like. Sure, we have shit going on, but we're doing our best to keep our game faces on, especially since there are kids here. We don't want them knowin' we're all a bit stressed.

It's your typical Saturday night. Brothers are gathered around the fire with either their ol' ladies on their laps or a clubwhore to keep them warm for the night. The pornstars who work for the club are here too, enjoying the low-key evening.

For the first time in a while, we have visitors. Boss, the Prez of the Iron Vex MC, is here. She brought her daughter, Destiny. Her ol' man, Cowboy, tagged along with her. Destiny and Ace are playing off closer to the water, with Riva, our enforcer's ol' lady watching the two of them. Hell, we didn't even know if Ace was ever gonna be able to have a normal life, but here she is, actin' like a lil' girl should.

Mammoth sits a few feet to my right on a severed tree stump. We have a few stumps around the fire for us to sit on when we want. A bit redneck if you ask me, but it works. "It's good to see that lil' one with a smile on her face. I didn't know if we were ever gonna see this," Mammoth speaks up, and I nod in agreement.

Every single one of us here loves Ace like she's our own daughter, but her father, or rather her biological father, is a disgusting piece of shit who deserves to be where he is—six feet under. We don't speak his name and we all celebrated when Gamble told us he took his last breath. I can attest for most of us when I say I hope we could've had a round at him. He took so much from us, including my best friend, Dog. He was the Prez before he was killed by Ace's biological father. Then Gamble was made Prez as a joke, and the rest is history.

"It was a close one," I comment to Mammoth, eyes on the little girl with blonde curly hair like her momma.

Mammoth clears his throat. "Mhm. You seen any of them Beasts of Brutality lately?"

I glance to my right and see his eyes are locked onto mine. He's worried. I wouldn't say I'm worried, more like I'm cautious, but as long as we don't stir up too much trouble, we should be fine. "No, not since the last time."

"I don't like how close they are, Ravage. They're too close to us. You know it'll only bring trouble."

Hell, their club name is confirmation enough of his statement. "For now, we sit back and assess the situation. We can't act recklessly."

"If we do, it'll only make things worse," Hart, Gamble's ol' man, speaks up from my left. He walks over to Mammoth and me with the same tight-lipped expression that he's always sporting.

"We know who they are, which only makes things worse. We know what they're capable of," I state, crossing my arms, I lean back a bit, trying to relax my tense muscles, but it doesn't work.

"We can take them. They can't be worse than others we've faced before," Mammoth speaks up.

Hart scoffs, "They're some of Rage's worst. They won't be easy to deal with and that's a promise."

"You talkin' about the Beasts of Brutality?" a voice questions from behind us. I turn my head to look back, seein' Boss' ol' man, Cowboy. He's not only her man but the Prez of her Boston, Massachusetts charter.

With a beer in hand, he approaches, and Hart takes over, leading the conversation. "You've heard of them?"

Cowboy scoffs, unable to hide his disgust. "Hits a bit closer to home, I'm afraid. Two of my blood brothers are part of the club."

I crane my neck, watching how Cowboy reacts *very* carefully. I should give the guy some credit, but I don't know enough about him. He might not have a good relationship with his brothers. Then again, he could be playin' us somehow. There's not a stone I'll leave unturned. Not after goin' through the shit we all have here.

"What's the deal with that?" Hart doesn't waste time as he asks his question. All of us assume the worst until proven otherwise. It's just the way things go here. You don't automatically get trust. You *earn* it.

Cowboy takes a swig of his beer before taking a moment before he speaks. "Duke and Pistol were my brothers before they chose this path. They're fucked up. They're . . . repulsive. There isn't much to tell where they're concerned. I have a family now, and that's my priority," Cowboy states, looking over to where Boss and Gamble are chatting, and then his eyes dart over to Destiny. While he isn't the girl's birth father, you'd never know. He's stepped up in every sense of the word.

"C'mon, you have to give us more than that," Hart grumbles, glaring at Cowboy.

Cowboy shakes his head. "If you want me to tell you everything will be fine while they're around, I won't. They're sick fucks who don't know when to stop. My advice? Take them out while you can so all of you can sleep better at night."

Hart looks over to Mammoth and me, and we know. We're unable to escape the shit that keeps following us. Whenever we think we're finally able to get a breath, reality comes crashing in.

Trouble and issues will always be close by. It's become our way of life.

MARISOLE

My vision is blurry as I open my eyes. It takes a few minutes for everything to become clear again, and as it does, I realize where I am. Not going to lie, I thought I'd be in Hell for taking my own life and all, but even the flames of Hell wouldn't burn as badly as my tears do now.

I'm on Scar's deep blue comforter and the posters on the wall prove I'm in the very place I didn't want to be. I wasn't successful. God, why am I here?

Why am I still here if only to live a life of pain? It doesn't make any sense to me. None of this does.

My husband makes me constantly feel like I can't do anything right. God forbid I take a breath wrong. The next moment I have his fist closing in on my cheek. This life of mine is hardly life at all. It's more of a prison.

Pushing my hands underneath me, I pull myself up on the bed and look to the bedside table. Sweat beads across my forehead and nausea rolls through my stomach. I don't have any idea how long I've been out. It could've been hours, or maybe even days.

A spoon lays beside the syringe, and I pull open the drawer to the nightstand. Sure enough, a baggy with my heroin is there, and my lighter is right where I last left it. Scar deals drugs around this area, so he always makes sure to have a good stock for him and his guys. The night I married him, he held me down and injected me with what he called his best stuff. Since then, I can't remember a day where I haven't taken a hit.

I grab the spoon, put some powder in it, and light the lighter underneath it. All I need is a couple of minutes to liquify this, allow it to cool down for a couple minutes, and then get it in the syringe. Then I'll be close to my high, closer to not feeling a fucking thing anymore.

After I get the heroin melted down and give it a couple of minutes to cool, I search desperately for my tourniquet. It isn't where I last left it, so I look around, sure enough finding it on the floor between the side of my bed and the night table. Picking it up, I wrap it around my left arm and tie it off, keeping my arm one with gravity. It's the easiest way I've found I can get a vein.

My high is closer than ever, so I grab the syringe and pull on the opposite end, so the rose gold liquid goes in. I bring it to my arm and look for a vein but finding one has become an issue over the last few months.

I use my middle finger against my thumb and flick at the crook of my arm. After a couple moments, a vein pops up and I insert the needle. As I pull back the plunger, I know I've hit a vein, so I inject the heroin into my body. Once all of it is inside, I pull off the tourniquet and remove the needle, tossing it in the trash can next to my bed.

Leaning back against the pillows, I breathe in and out slowly while the numbness goes over every part of my body. I don't feel anymore. I don't hurt. I don't know *anything*. I'm just here.

If my father was still alive, I wonder if he would've let Scar get away with this. If he would've allowed him to turn me into this drug-ridden, pathetic excuse of a human. On the day of my wedding, my father never showed. He promised he was going to walk me down the aisle and be there for me. I, being the gullible girl I was, believed every lie and promise he said to me.

Scar told me a week after our wedding that he'd

been taken and was killed. How there was an auction and everything. It gutted me. I knew my father was never going to come in and get me out of this horrible situation and that I was stuck dealing with it myself. Truthfully, I should've tried to kill myself ages ago. I don't know why I waited nine years to do it. I can't understand why I waited this long, not that it matters since I'm still here.

Intense euphoria begins to take hold of me as the drugs storm through my veins. The door to my bedroom opens and the only way I can tell is from the sudden surge of light. It becomes dark yet again and the light on the bedside table illuminates part of the room.

His chiseled jaw comes into view, and then I spot the monarch butterfly tattoo on the side of his neck— my husband—Scar.

He snorts, "You thought you could leave me? You won't ever leave. Not now. Not ever. I'll give you all the drugs you need to be with me, but you're *never* going to get away from me, you pathetic bitch." He tugs at my leggings and pulls them down, flips me over, and the *clink* of his belt tells me what's about to happen. It's the only thing he ever uses me for.

A surge of cold air hits my ass and he uses his hands to spread my pussy lips before slamming his cock inside me. He doesn't care if I'm aroused in the least bit. Scar only cares about himself.

Heat comes beside my ear and he grits out his words, "I won't ever let you die, and that's a promise."

He rocks his dick in and out of me until he's finished. Hot spurts of his cum hit my ass and the pressure that was once there is gone.

The bed rises as he slides off and he heads for the door. Light comes into the room for a moment and Scar speaks up, "She's just taken a hit if anyone wants a round with my wife."

Without the drugs, I don't know how I'd be able to bear any of this.

CHAPTER FOUR

RAVAGE

"You've got ten more minutes, girls, then we need to pack up and leave!" Boss yells over to Destiny and Ace, who're making a sandcastle together. Ace draws her brows together and glares at Boss, proving yet again she's got Gamble's attitude. Destiny, on the other hand, continues packing sand in the stone indented pail, acting like she hasn't even heard her mother.

It's been a few days since Boss and Cowboy have been here with Destiny. Now they'll be heading back to Queens in the morning, and then the following day, Cowboy will be going back to Boston to check in and see how his club is doing.

The sun is starting to set and the sky's now a mixture of orange, pink, and purple. We've spent most of the day in the sun, relaxing as much as we can, hoping none of us would catch wind of those Beasts of Brutality fuckers. Hell, we made sure to surround not only Gamble, Hart, and Ace, but Destiny, Boss, and Cowboy too. Riva and Mammoth stuck in the center with their little girl, Dahlia. She's about three months old now and any chance Riva can get, she's showin' that little one of hers off.

Judge sinks back in the beach chair a few feet to my right and groans. "What I wouldn't kill for a couple of ice-cold beers."

"You want some? Fuck it, let's go to the boardwalk and find a bar. There's bound to be somethin' around here," I tell him, rising from the chair.

Judge cocks a brow and pulls his sunglasses down the bridge of his nose. "You fuckin' with me or what? They're gonna overcharge the fuck outta us."

"Aren't you the bastard who told me there's three things we don't underpay for in life? Drugs, pussy, and alcohol," I point out, knowin' for a fact it was Judge.

He cackles lightly and nods, gets up from his chair, and folds it down. I do the same to mine and we both head over to where Gamble and Hart are. "Hey, we're gonna go grab a drink. We'll toss the chairs in the back of Judge's truck and catch ya back at the club."

"Sure, just be careful. We're really close to Lewes

and I'm worried they're gonna turn up at any minute,"
Gamble says, her eyes looking past the two of us.

"If they do, we'll handle it. The two of us gotta
change anyway. I got my goods in the truck if you
know what I mean," I tell them. Now, I'd never bring a
gun onto a beach, but it doesn't mean I don't have my
shit in the truck if I need it. You can never be too
prepared in life.

"I'm following. Enjoy your night, both of you,"
Gamble says and waves her hand in dismissal. She'll be
leaving the beach in a few minutes anyway.

I tighten my grip around the aluminum chair and
lead the way back to the truck. Judge follows close
behind and once we're up the stairs, we cross the boardwalk, and the truck is parked in an alley. I toss my chair
in the bed and click the unlock button on the remote.
By the time Judge puts his chair in the back, I already
have the door open and I'm throwin' on a gray t-shirt.

Before we left the club, I threw a pair of black jeans
in a duffle bag with a light gray t-shirt and my cut. I
glance around lookin' for a bathroom within sight but
don't see one. Fuck it. I kick off my sandals and pull
down my trunks, lettin' my balls hit the breeze.

"Oh, hello there," a woman's sultry voice says as
she's walkin' by with a couple of her friends. They're
all smiles, but I'm sure they are after seein' a dick of

my size. Maybe I should stop them and offer it up. Hell, they might take a ride or two on it.

Judge looks over and covers his eyes up immediately. "What the fuck, man?! You tryin' to get arrested for indecent exposure?"

By the time he finishes asking his question, I'm zipping my jeans and sliding my belt through the hooks. "Now, that would be the highlight of my week. It's been a bit boring around here, hasn't it?" I look over to Judge, and he's shakin' his head, not able to put up with me right now.

I toss the sandals in the duffle bag, pull out my socks and boots and finish getting changed. Lastly, I slide my cut on and turn around to find Judge isn't anywhere in sight.

Well, I guess he got bored of waitin' around for me. I look around the street and don't really see anywhere he could've gone. Hell, if I'd seen a restroom sign, I would've changed there, not flashed my goods to all of Rehoboth.

A flash of copperish brown hair pulls my attention to the boardwalk, and I have to blink a couple of times, but by the time I resonate with who, I believe I just saw she's gone.

I dig into my jeans pocket and click the lock button on Judge's truck, walk up to the boardwalk and follow where I last saw her. Thank goodness the guy gave me his extra set of keys.

She doesn't look the same at all, but I swear it's her, or maybe a doppelgänger. I don't know where the fuck Judge is, but I'm not lookin' to stick around. If it's really her, I want to get closer. I spot another flash of the copperish brown hair and round the alley where she just walked down. I stick close to the corner of the building, hiding most of my body and I'm sure I look like a real creeper.

She walks down the alley and heads over to a bike. The guy's too far off for me to get a good look at him, but the emblem on his cut is easily visible from here. She's going up to the Beasts of Brutality MC.

She turns her head to look at me, and I get confirmation.

Marisole is here.

She's in Delaware.

I take a step back and inhale sharply just as Judge comes up, fully changed. "Where the hell did you go, man?"

"I could ask you the same fuckin' thing," I snap. Pushing past him, I head back toward the beach.

Gamble's still in her chair and I waste no time making my way down to her. Walkin' on the sand with combat boots on is fuckin' stupid as shit, but I need to tell her about this.

"Prez, we got a problem," I tell Gamble, and she immediately turns to look at me.

"Alright."

"Beasts of Brutality were just here."

"Okay . . ." Gamble narrows her eyes in on me and looks over at Judge. "Did something else happen?"

Fuck. I thought I was holdin' in my anger enough, but I guess not. "I saw my ex with them, alright?"

Gamble blinks a few times while she processes what I just said. "Well, shit. This is adding more to our plates . . . you're supposed to be leaving tomorrow with Needles. Are you still going with him, or do I need to send someone else?"

We've been tracking Konstantin down for months, so there's no way I'm going to miss the opportunity to make that bastard suffer for shooting a child, and I mean *suffer*. The man won't be able to breathe without feeling immense pain.

"No, I'm going. I wouldn't miss it for the world."

CHAPTER FIVE

MARISOLE

I can't believe I just . . . I mean, I don't even know if it was Ravage. It could've just been a guy who looked like him. I don't know. But what I do know is it was enough to scare me off from meeting one of Scar's guys for a trade. Scar has me do it from time to time, but not too often. Ever since the other day, he's barely left me out of his sight. Scar makes sure I keep myself doped-up so I don't feel anything and if he can't be with me, he makes sure one of the guys in the club is.

I sit back on the chair in the bedroom I share with Scar and my phone vibrates on the nightstand. I grab it and my half-sister's name pops up on the screen. I haven't met Rosa yet, but Xavier gave me her phone number and vice versa after he found her. Apparently, my father had more children than just me. We're all bastards, considering he never married anyone of importance . . . but not one of us knew about the other.

Rosa and I have a half-brother named Ricardo, and Xavier's been trying to locate him for a while now. Unfortunately, he keeps coming up short. Ricardo is constantly on the move, from what Xavier has said, so it explains why it's been so difficult for him to find my brother.

It just shows me how my life isn't what I thought it would be at all. Not in the least bit. When my father told me he arranged a marriage, I naturally assumed it was to someone of importance. Not a man like Scar. Most of what my father ended up telling me was a lie or a twisted way to get me to do what he wanted. At the end of the day, the only truthful thing he told me is something that still hurts me to this day.

He paid my mother so she wouldn't abort me.

I questioned her on it after he told me, and she confirmed she never wanted to be a mother. She wanted to run around and party, so my father paid her a million dollars to give birth to me and then paid her two-hundred-and-fifty thousand dollars a year until I was eighteen. I know people say there isn't a value on one's life, but my father gave me one. It just happens to be 5.5 million.

"Hey," I tell her the second I answer the phone.

"Hey there! I wasn't sure you'd pick up the phone. The last couple of times I called you didn't." I don't know Rosa very well, but I'm a quick learner. She tends to have a habit of slyly making you feel guilty for your actions in the past. I'm sure it works great on her boyfriend, but it fucking sucks when you're her sister.

I didn't even know my siblings existed. I only knew about them when Xavier showed up here a couple months ago. Man, it threw Scar off. He thought I called Xavier, but I didn't. Hell, I didn't even have a way to get in contact with the man. It's not like one of the brothers in Scar's club would've given me their phone to reach out to him. No way.

Long story short, Xavier told Scar and me about my brother and sister and how he gave Rosa a heads up about what our dear old dad had planned for her. He gave us the rundown on how Rosa would only get her inheritance if she married a Bolivian drug lord, but she didn't. After all that, he told me how my sister wanted to have a relationship with me. He wanted to give me her phone number, but I didn't have a phone and I made him aware of the mere fact.

I know now Scar will never let me die, but on that day, I thought I was going to. Scar slapped me around, shoved me into walls, and beat me with a whip for telling Xavier what he deemed was our business.

"Sorry, things have been a bit crazy over here." I lie through my teeth, hoping my sister won't dig. We're still learning about each other and I haven't told her my husband is the Prez of an MC club. Xavier told me she's with the Reapers Rejects MC and when we found that out, Scar's disposition changed immediately, and it wasn't in a good way.

It made me think the club she's involved in isn't friendly with Scar, so I've kept things very hush-hush. I don't want to create problems, so I tell her a little bit about me every time we talk and she knows I live in Lewes, Delaware. Otherwise, she doesn't have a clue.

"Oh? What's going on down there?" Rosa immediately questions.

Fuck, I didn't think this through. "Oh, you know, just a busy time of year." I keep it plain and simple, hoping it's enough for her to accept.

"I bet it's crazy. Always is around the beaches, right?"

"Right," I confirm.

Rosa clears her throat. "So, I was talking to Axel and we think it would be a good idea if we finally meet. We have been talking for a couple months at this point and don't you think it's time we see each other? I mean, hell, we both have so many years to make up for."

I know this is a moment where my heart should

swell, but instead, it sinks into the pit of my stomach and I struggle to find the words.

Heavy footsteps begin to come closer to me, so I hang up the phone and hide it under my pillow. Scar's broad shoulders fill the doorframe as the door's pushed open and he walks inside, but he isn't alone. There's another man behind him. He has blond hair like Scar does, but it's lighter, almost a snow-like color. He has piercing blue eyes that remind you of the ocean and his skin is pale, like a Viking.

The man scoffs and immediately looks displeased with Scar. "This is how you expect to pay your debt? One time with her? No." The man turns and begins to walk out of the bedroom, but Scar clears his throat, causing the man in the suit to turn and look at him.

"What is it? I have things to do."

"You have a weekend with her. Not one day. A weekend. You can pimp her out, do whatever you fuckin' want, I don't care. All I care about is that we make things good between us." Scar seems desperate and his worries lace his voice. This man might not know my husband well enough to read him, but I do.

The man takes a step into the bedroom and his eyes rake over my body. I'm wearing a blue spaghetti strap top and a pair of shorts. I don't look decent in the least bit.

"Stand up," the blond man orders, so I look at my

husband, who nods. Over the years, I've learned to only do as Scar says, not anyone else.

I scoot myself off the bed and stand up, staring at the man who has eyes that can very well look through me. He goes around Scar and circles my body, his eyes feeling like lasers on my skin.

He hooks a finger and slides it underneath the strap of my shirt and begins to tug down until he immediately stops. He clicks his tongue against the roof of his mouth and waves his finger in a naughty motion at Scar. "I see the track marks, Scar. She's no good to me or to work an event. Do you understand? I expect to be paid in full, not with your doped-up wife. It could've worked if she wasn't riddled with these. Shit, if you give a fuck about her, then you'll get her off this shit. Our business is done here. You have two weeks." The man leaves the bedroom and shuts the door behind him, and the next thing I know, Scar has his hand around my neck.

"Why do you have to be such a worthless cunt, huh!?" he snarls in my face, shoving me against the wall. My back cracks at the impact and Scar whips out his knife from his jeans, flips it open, and presses the blade against my throat. I inhale slowly through my nose, knowing he won't kill me. If he did, it would be a blessing. He only wishes to hurt me, to make me feel the pain as much as I can. Scar gets off on punishing me.

He presses the blade against my throat even further until a burning sensation starts just below my jawbone. Warmth slowly cascades down my neck and even if I wanted to glance down, I can't. It'll only make more blood come.

My phone vibrates under the pillow and I pray Scar doesn't go for it, but I make the mistake of looking at my pillow and his attention immediately shifts. Still, with the knife pressed to my throat, he uses his other hand to toss my pillow on the other side of the bed and sees the phone ringing.

"Well, looks like sissy dearest is calling." He cackles lowly, swipes left, and answers the phone. Scar quickly puts it on speaker so I can hear every bit of the conversation. "Rosa, Marisole is busy right now. Can she call you back later?"

There's a few moments of silence before my sister speaks. "What? I was just talking to her and catching up. What do you mean—"

"I needed her to do something for me, so she had to go handle that. I'll get her to call you back later." Scar taps the red button on the screen and ends the call. He tosses the phone on my bed and takes a step closer to me. His chest is brushing against mine and the blade is severing more of my skin. The burning is only getting worse, and God, I want it to stop. I don't want this life, not if this is what the rest of my days are going to be like.

Though, I'm the only person to blame for the way things worked out.

I could've made an entirely different decision all those years ago—one where I'd be happy.

"What the fuck were you telling your sister?" Scar demands an answer from me and uneasiness settles into my gut. The night is only going to get worse, so much worse.

RAVAGE

The flight to the Ukraine felt like we walked here. Everyone at the Knights of Retribution MC is ready for us to make Konstantin pay for what he did, and now we're closer than ever. Probably why this feels like it's taken forever. There's so much ridin' on Needles and me, and the pressure is on.

Konstantin almost killed Ace. The sick bastard shot her in the head as a way to hurt Ace's biological father . . . but it wouldn't have hurt him in the least bit. When he was alive, it's not even like he gave a fuck. Hell, he had multiple people rape Gamble at a club meeting in Louisiana. Then you add in Ace getting shot? It's no wonder we left the Royal Bastards and the Knights of

Retribution were reborn again. Shit was getting crazier by the fuckin' day.

"Are you ready for this?" Needles shouldn't even be asking this question. Of course, I'm ready. We're both ready.

I give him a knowing look and he nods, and the two of us leave the shitty little hotel room we're renting for the night. We've been here for two hours already and even though we're exhausted beyond measure, we need to get things done quickly.

Kiev is one of Ukraine's most popular cities. Not only is it Ukraine's capital, but it's also where many people around the world come to do business, travel, so on and so forth. The original plan was for Needles to call in a couple of the guys he served with, but Gamble thought it was better if we handled this in-house, and I agree. The fewer people who know, the better.

We were able to use our friend, Ion Petran's private jet. He's the head of the Romanian mafia and is one of our strongest allies. Luckily, the Romanian's believe family goes above all else too. When Ion heard what happened to Ace, the man wanted vengeance too. Anything he could've helped with, he has.

Ion even has a sort of connection with Konstantin. One of his head clan member's wife used to be a very prominent gang leader here in the Ukraine. She still has connections here and personally knows Konstantin. Ion had her call Konstantin and arrange a meeting. Now, there's only one thing this man wants more of —*power*.

Vera was able to get Konstantin to agree to meet her at a building owned by the Romanian mafia. Only, it isn't solely her that he'll end up meeting. Instead, it'll be Vera, Needles, and myself.

I cannot wait for this man to get what's coming to him. It's been a long time coming and I know Gamble would've wanted to be here herself, but given everything happening in Delaware, we'd be foolish to put her at more risk.

The building we're in is a condominium complex. I don't know the specifics on which one of the Romanian mafia members owns this, but none of those details matter. The only important thing is that Konstantin gets here.

Ion's handling the cleanup as a favor to the club and personally, it's a bit weird to me. In my eyes, you can't trust anyone . . . but Gamble trusts him and we have to follow her lead.

Needles and I get in the back of a taxi and head over to the condominium complex. It takes about fifteen minutes for us to get to the complex and the moment our driver stops in front of the doors, we exit and I give him a nice tip. Not too nice, though. I don't want him to remember us.

Needles and I walk in through the lobby and a man greets us behind the receptionist's desk. He's wearing an all-black suit and smiles brightly the moment he spots us. "Good evening, gentlemen. How may I be of service to you?"

I take a step forward and keep my expression tight-lipped. "Ion sent us here, told us to ask for Glib."

Immediately his expression falters and I can visibly see a wave of worry wash over him. "Glib, you say? Please wait here while I go get him." The man goes back behind his desk, pushes open a door, and leaves Needles and me in the lobby.

"Shit, this is a fancy joint," Needles tells me, his eyes scanning the entire lobby, but as they stop, I try to find what he's focused on. "They have cameras."

"It doesn't matter. Today they're having technical difficulties, so nothing is working, stopped a few hours ago." I fake a frown, and Needles chuckles.

"Shit, I'm glad you said so. What's the deal with this place, given you know." I'm the guy who has most of the information. Always have been since my entire world was rocked in my early twenties. Before then, I wasn't the type who paid attention to much or was even receptive now that I think about it.

"They rent this place to businessmen coming into

Kiev for weeks or months at a time. It's all I know. I didn't ask for details that don't pertain to our visit here."

"Understood," Needles comments with a nod.

The door behind the desk opens and the man who greeted us when we arrived comes through. "Glib will be here in a moment."

He goes behind his computer and taps away on the screen, presumably finishing work. Needles and I stand in the lobby, speaking amongst ourselves while we wait, and the door opens behind the receptionist again. A man with broad shoulders fills the frame of the door. He looks like he's the one the mafia sends to collect a debt—the type of man who doesn't let anyone get away with shit.

"Come with me," Glib commands with a thick Ukrainian accent and we immediately follow. Needles widens his eyes as Glib leads us down a long, dark hallway and makes a left. We go from seeing rooms and numbers every once and a while to nothing. "This room, it has an uh, how do you say in English? Reputation. Yes, a reputation. Many with power know this is where the high-class women will meet for eh . . . sexual transactions."

Perfect. This is how we're going to get him. He won't know what hit him. Not now, not ever.

Now, all we do is wait.

Only a few more minutes of waiting and justice will be served.

CHAPTER SEVEN

MARISOLE

I stir awake, fluttering my eyelids open as Breaking Benjamin's "Angel's Fall" plays from the stereo behind me. My entire body aches, muscles feeling like I've been beaten repeatedly. My head pounds and I'm freezing. I move my arms to my sides and push myself up. The soreness on my thighs pulsates through my muscles as I try to pull myself off the pool table. I'm able to get to the side and as I scoot myself down, stars fill my vision.

The next thing I know, I'm waking up on the floor. I inhale slowly, not understanding why I'm so weak. Hell, I don't even know what day it is. How long has it been since the phone call with my sister?

I blink rapidly, opening my eyes and see more

track marks on my arm. I don't remember taking any hits, but it's not the first time I've blacked out. Not that Scar hasn't done the hard work for me. If he thinks I'm being too much of a problem, he'll dope me up. One time I overdosed because of his ass. He bought product from some other dude and obviously, it was laced with some shit. Fucking idiot.

Reaching a hand up, I grab onto the side of the pool table and pull myself up. The soft fabric brushes against the pads of my fingers as I force myself to stand. The stars fill my vision yet again and I do my best to keep myself steady.

Taking the trip to the bedroom is terrifying, knowing if I make one wrong step, I'll plummet down to the ground. Not one of the brothers here offer to help me to the bedroom, but why would they? Scar gets off on this type of shit.

I lose my footing as I reach the dark hallway, grasping the wall like it'll help me stay upright. A warm hand comes around the back of my neck and I'm turned around abruptly. Duke's dark eyes bore into mine and a grimace pulls at his lips. "I wasn't done with you yet, sweetheart," he sneers, slapping my thigh, so I open my legs up for him.

I do as he commands, swallowing hard as more stars fill my vision. I weave to the left and he ends up catching me so I don't hit the ground. "Fuck, you're jacked up bad tonight, girl. Guess I'll have to throw you down on the bed. Don't need you to do much of anythin' except empty my balls," Duke grumbles, his tone full of displeasure.

I'm hoisted up into his arms and he carries me through the rest of the hallway until he reaches the door. Duke turns the knob and pushes it open and the stars overtake my vision. The next thing I know, I'm on the bed and who I assume is Duke is grinding his cock inside me. My pussy burns, knowing the man didn't use anything. Fuck, did I pass out again? I must've.

"Aw, yes," Duke hisses as he slams into me even harder. "Fuck, yes, take that cum."

I act like I'm asleep, just taking it, knowing when he's done, he'll leave. Duke pulls out of me and the clinking of his belt tells me he's about to leave. I continue to stay on the bed, breathing in and out slowly until the door is slammed shut from behind.

I grab onto the comforter and pull myself up, sit on the bed and put my back against the wall. My naked body looks . . . disgusting. I can see my ribs, my bones are clearly visible in my arms, and my decent rack is now part of the itty-bitty-titty committee.

Buzzing comes from the left and I glance over, seeing Rosa's name pop up on the screen. Immediately, I answer. "Rosa," I say her name in a breathless whisper.

"Marisole, God, I haven't heard from you in days. We're on our way. I just need to know where you are."

She's on what? "What did you say?" I question, needing further reiteration.

"Axel and I, we're on our way to Delaware right now. You really freaked me out and I'll be there tonight. Okay? We're almost there, so just keep doing what you're doing."

"Rosa . . . what . . ." I don't know how the hell I'm supposed to tell her not to come here. She doesn't need to come in and be my knight in shining whatever. "You can't come here. If you do, things will only get worse."

Rosa scoffs, "Yeah, well, they sound pretty bad to begin with. I know you don't know me. Hell, we barely know each other, but we're sisters. It's our job to keep each other safe. So, I'm coming whether you like it or not."

"Rosa, *please*, I'm begging you. Don't come here. If you do . . . if you do, I'm afraid what . . ." I don't even know what to say other than I'm afraid. I don't think Scar will kill me, but then again, I don't know why he's kept me around for this long either.

"The mere fact you're afraid is why you need to

leave. It's not safe, Marisole. You know it and so do I. If you don't leave, you're going to die there."

"I can't just leave."

"Sure you can. The man doesn't own you. I get you're married. I get our father arranged this for you, but I'm sure even he wouldn't want you in a marriage like this. You're a Ramirez, Marisole. In Mexico, that name means something. Women like us don't become victims and if you stay, you're allowing this to happen. So, I'm giving you an out. I'm giving you this one shot to leave his ass. You won't have to do it alone. I'll be there by your side. Axel and his club, they'll back us up."

Inhaling deeply, I know in my heart this is the right choice. This is the opportunity I've waited a lifetime for, so I rattle off the address and end the call.

I'm going to get out of this mess. I never thought it would be possible, but now I'm closer than ever.

CHAPTER EIGHT

RAVAGE

The modern clock ticks on the wall and I watch the hand move as the seconds go by. Konstantin was supposed to be here fifteen minutes ago. My blood boils under my skin at the thought we're being stood up. Does he know this is an elaborate scheme to get him here? Could he know what the plan is? So many questions storm through my head.

Glib, one of Ion's henchmen, runs and operates the condominium complex. He personally assured me he'd bring Konstantin back to us once he arrived. I figured he was telling the truth given the way he looked angered when discussing the man, but now I'm not sure.

"Where the fuck is this fool at?" Needles impatiently asks, pacing the room.

I look back at him and shrug. "No idea, man, but gettin' all riled up won't help shit. You know it."

Needles is ex-special ops. He knows how this goes. You wait it out and pray things go to plan. But him bein' nervous as can be, isn't helpin' me at all. Inhaling deeply through my nose, I walk across the room and look out through the window into the private garden. It's too classy for me, but what the hell? We'll make it work for the time being.

In Kiev it's raining and the sky is becoming darker by the moment. Fitting for what I hope is still about to unfold today. Needles and I are only here for the night, so we need to work fast. The latch on the door clicks, signaling someone is here. Footsteps come closer to us, growing heavier with every step. "Vera, I was so glad you called. Now, what is it we can discuss?" Konstantin starts off, though he realizes soon enough Vera isn't here.

"I gotta ask you a question, man. You always been this fucked up, or is it somethin' that you turned into?" Needles asks him, malice laced through his voice.

I pull my hunting knife from my pocket and open it. Fuck, I love the way it glimmers. I just bought it from a pawn shop in Seaford. They got some intense shit in there for firearms and knives. I'm gonna have to take the brothers there when I get back. I promised Butcher I'd show him around the joint.

Konstantin immediately tenses while his eyes search for an answer. "C'mon, you don't know us? You don't recognize our faces, or these?" I ask, pulling on my cut as I cut the distance between us. He turns and pulls the gun from his holster, but I'm too quick for him. I smack it from his hands.

Needles has his gun pulled and he's pointing it right at Konstantin. "Don't you get trigger happy. He's got too much to pay for."

"Where is Vera?" Konstantin asks, looking between Needles and me.

"Come on, you can't honestly tell me you don't know what's going on here. Don't you recognize me?" I pull on my cut and Konstantin looks over me. He probably won't recognize shit. When he came after us, it was when we were part of the Royal Bastards MC.

Konstantin doesn't say a fuckin' word. I don't hold back my grimace. I grab him by his suit jacket and shove him against the floor. Lifting my leg, I waste no time kicking him in the face and a loud *pop* comes the second my boot collides with his face.

Blood pours from his nose onto the white tiles below us and he desperately tries to wipe it away. "What the fuck!? Who are you!?"

Kneeling down, I grab him by the throat and drag

my knife against the side of his face, slicing him slowly. I want to make sure he feels *every* bit of this. He tries to shove at me and get away, but he won't. What he did is unspeakable. He broke every code we have. You never go after family and you especially never hurt children.

"You shot her in the head and she almost died because of you," I sneer, digging the blade deeper into his flesh. He turns his head to the left and the right, further cutting himself. I can't help but smile at the misery he's causing himself.

"No, you have the wrong man!" he claims, but Needles and I know it isn't true.

"You were trying to hurt the Royal Bastards and you shot a baby. What kind of sick, twisted fuck does that?" Needles growls, coming closer to Konstantin. I pull my blade back and shove him to the ground again, kicking him another time in the face for good measure. He screams in agony as my boot makes contact with his nose, and I take a couple steps back so Needles can get a round in with him.

Konstantin scoffs and smirks in a devilish manner as blood floods over his teeth and lips. "Rancid's kid? Who gives a fuck? Better off dead if you ask me."

Needles doesn't hold back, not in the least bit. He grabs his knife, pulls it out, and goes to town on Konstantin. He's punching holes into his body like he's a balloon that needs to be popped. There's no regard or respect for life here. Not after what Konstantin did, and we'll never accept him.

"Don't kill him, yet. I want to make sure he suffers," I warn Needles, and he stands up, backs away a few steps and nods. He doesn't want to stop, but he'll respect the order I just gave him.

I grab Konstantin by the neck and tighten my grip around his throat. "You will never hurt anyone else again, and we're here to make sure you regret ever pulling that trigger."

His eyes widen in fear and I know he sees how serious I am. I'd love to be in this room and torture him for hours, days, and even weeks on end . . . but we have a flight leaving in the morning. Our time is limited, so we'd better make it worth it.

By the time we're boarding the plane back to the States, I know I'll be able to sleep a bit easier, knowing this man isn't breathing the same air as we are.

CHAPTER NINE

MARISOLE

"Bring her out here right now!" a woman's voice screeches from the top of her lungs, loud enough to cause me to wake from my hazy state.

Deep, throaty laughter rings down the hallway through my open door.

Blinking, I force my eyes open and glance down to find a needle in my arm. I don't even remember injecting myself, but it wouldn't be the first time I've gotten high and didn't remember. Fuck, it's not like Scar or his boys haven't done it to me before. One time I developed an abscess under the skin because Pistol wanted to have his way with me. That guy is just . . . he's *too* rough, so whenever he comes around, I do tend to put up a fight. I don't with the others, though. I guess it's 'cause I know what my life is like here. I've accepted it, but most of the guys don't treat me the way Pistol does.

I take the syringe from my arm and toss it in the trash can, put my alternate hand over where the needle was and push hard. While I do this, I scoot off the side of the bed and my bare feet hit the ground with a *thud*.

"What're you fucking laughing at, you twisted piece of shit," the woman's voice grows more venomous with every word, and as she continues to speak, I realize I've heard this voice before.

"Oh, nothin'. It's just entertainin' how you think you can waltz into my club and demand shit, especially my wife. She belongs to me. I don't give a fuck if she's your sister or not."

Wait . . . could this be who I think it is?

"Let me make this crystal clear for you, man, we're not leavin' without her sister. My ol' lady will put lead in every one of your boys here until she gets what she wants, and I'll fuckin' back her up," a man's voice declares. His tone is deep and authoritative, but bits of attitude shoot through his words.

I make my way down the narrow hallway and round the corner, holding onto the corner as dizziness starts to consume me. At the sight of her deep, sea-green hair, I'm blown away. It's Rosa. My sister is here.

With widened eyes, I'm unable to stop looking at her. It's the first time I've seen her, but we look so much alike. We have the same nose and dark eyes, even the same cheekbones . . . there's not a doubt in my mind we're related. Before, I did have doubts. My father lied to me so much, and I don't trust Xavier at all. This could've been another one of his elaborate lies or schemes.

The man standing next to her is ripped as can be. Tattoos cover his arms, and he's wearing a cut like Scar does, but instead of being part of a shitty club like this, he's part of a decent one. He has to be Axel, her ol' man. She's told me great things about him, but now I see what she means. He's her number one supporter and it shows.

Pistol stands beside my husband and glares at Axel. "Prez, we really gonna let these two fuckheads keep talkin' or end 'em right where they stand?"

Scar looks at Pistol and he's debating what to do, but the moment the door to the club comes flying open and one of Scar's boys hits the ground like a sack of potatoes, he jumps up from his seat. "What the fuck?!" my husband roars, glaring at the man in the doorway.

"Shit, Scar . . . I thought you were fuckin' dead. Hadn't heard you were still stirrin' up shit, but I should've known a snake-like you would still be slitherin' in the grass." The man putting my husband in his place demands attention. It's not only the way he speaks but his demeanor and the way he carries himself. Not an ounce of fear shows. He struts up, stepping over the man he tossed in here and four more men come funneling in behind him.

Scar's eyes shift to mine. "I didn't know you were this much trouble, Marisole."

"Give the girl over to her sister before we have to start throwin' lead around. You're a vile piece of shit, but you aren't stupid," the man states, keeping his eyes trained on my husband.

Scar glares at him, and I'm at a point where I don't know what he's going to do.

"Zane, back down. This isn't your fight. Unless you want to make an enemy of me?" Scar raises his eyebrows and walks closer to Zane. Meanwhile, Rosa crosses the room and comes up to me.

"What, you think you're scary? Think again, motherfucker," Zane sneers, and all of his guys take a couple steps in.

"Are you alright?" Rosa asks me quietly, her eyes filled with worry.

My hands shake as she wraps an arm around my back and holds onto my hip. "I told you not to come." Tears threaten to spill, but I'm trying so hard to keep my shit together. Her being here not only puts me in danger but her and her friends too. Scar is unpredictable. You can think things are fine and then a second later, he's got a knife to your neck or a bullet in you. Hell, I would know. I have firsthand experience.

"A man who threatens me has never stepped foot in my club and lived to tell the tale," Scar growls.

Zane, though, this man cackles in his face. "Good thing I'm fuckin' royalty, now, tell your bitches to let them pass, or I'll light this fuckin' joint up." Zane pulls out his gun and presses it between Scar's eyes.

Lord almighty. Is this really happening?

"They can leave on one condition," Scar says as he takes his gun and puts it down on the table. His nostrils flare and Zane puts his gun back in his holster.

Rosa slowly begins to walk me across the room and before I know it, Scar's headed straight for us. I watch as Axel and the guys tense up, all of them having a hand on their guns. He scrunches his nose in disgust as he speaks. "Is an addict really worth this much trouble?"

Without hesitation, my sister replies, "Damn straight, now get the fuck out of my way."

Scar takes a step back and my sister walks with me until we're through the door of the clubhouse. She walks me up to a massive diesel truck and gets me in on the passenger side. A bald man with a beard is behind the wheel. "Fuck, you look like you could use a donut. They got a Duck's around here? I mean, they gotta, right?"

"Marisole, this is Bull. Bull, this is Marisole, and yeah, I'm sure we can stop by one." Rosa rolls her eyes and looks to me. "Last time we were out here, he ordered two dozen sand donuts and ate them all himself."

"Whoa, don't you fuckin' fat shame me." Bull seems appalled by Rosa's words.

"And don't you be a dramatic bitch. Jesus, I wasn't fuckin' fat shamin' you." I scoot closer to Bull as my sister climbs in. Axel comes up behind her and speaks.

"I'll meet you at their club in a bit. Just get goin' and make sure no one is on your tail. Got it?"

"Sure do. Love you and be safe," Rosa says as Axel backs away, and she slams the door to the truck shut. Bull puts the truck in reverse and speeds out of here and as I let out the pent-up breath I've been holding, the reality hits me like a semi-truck . . . I'm out.

I got out.

RAVAGE

"God, I can't wait to get home and sink my—" Needles speaks up.

"Don't finish that fuckin' sentence, dude. I don't need to hear about what you do with Flora." I tell him, giving him a look that tells him a warning.

"Oh, come on. You know what she does for a livin'. Hell, you think I'm not the one makin' that pussy nice and wet before a scene with one of the girls?" A shit-eating smirk crosses Needles' face and I can't help but break out into laughter. He has no shame in his game, that's for fuckin' certain. "Hell, when's the last time you got laid?"

"That's none of your concern," I tell him, throwing my duffle bag over my shoulder as we walk out to the parking garage area. Ion's plane touched down in Philadelphia and it's about two in the morning right now. We're gonna crash at Riva's, Mammoth's ol' lady, place in the city. Her sisters, Astrid and Johanna, live there now, but they don't mind us crashing in the living room.

"That's what pent-up bastards say," Needles snickers while we cross the street. We called an Uber to meet us here, and sure enough, a Jeep Wrangler comes rolling up.

"You Tony?" I question the guy, and he nods.

"Yeah, where you boys headed?" he asks.

I give him the information while Needles and I hop in the back of his Wrangler. Hell, I should've grabbed the passenger seat. This shit is cramped in here. Not enough leg room at all. It's only about a ten-minute ride, so I bite my tongue and don't say shit. I finally turn my phone back on to see a message from Gamble. I tap on her name.

From: Gamble

Zane and a few of his boys from the Reapers Rejects are here. Just giving you a heads up. I'm having Butcher drive the truck to get you boys tomorrow at noon, so be ready to leave.

Shit. I wonder what went down while we were away.

To: Gamble

Alright. No problem. See you tomorrow.

I slide my cell back into my pants and the next few minutes fly by. Tony pulls up outside the apartment complex and we get out of his Jeep. We both have our duffle bags in tow and walk up to the door. We have to press on the apartment number and be buzzed up.

"Hello?" a woman with a thick Swedish accent answers.

"Hey, it's Ravage. Riva told you we were coming tonight."

"Oh yes, come on up," she quickly replies.

The door buzzes and we head on in, going upstairs to the number Riva gave us. "Shit, if any of 'em are hot, you should test one out. I can't for obvious reasons, but fuck dude, you're not tied down for shit."

I roll my eyes at Needles' suggestion, but the moment the apartment door opens and I see not just a brunette, but a blonde too . . . shit. It doesn't hurt. They both look like they could be models. The brunette is a bit curvier, while the blonde is thin. The blonde doesn't have tits, but she's got a nice lookin' ass from the way she's standing. The brunette one has a nice rack, though, and a nice ass.

"I'm surprised you two are awake," I murmur as we approach the door.

"We wanted to make sure you were welcomed. Hospitality is very important," the blonde one says before extending a hand. "I'm Astrid, and this is Johanna." She looks to the brunette, who smiles deviously, not moving her eyes from mine.

I'm old enough to know what women want and when they want it. Johanna seems the type who doesn't have a problem giving the signals, and I'll be receptive. Maybe Needles is right. Maybe it's about time I get my dick wet.

"Astrid is lying. She's heading out, as you can see." Johanna looks over at her sister. I didn't even pay much attention to her outfit. She's wearing a soft blue mini dress with knee-high boots. I don't know if it's suede, but it looks like a soft sort of material.

Astrid pushes past us and waves her hand. "Bye, nice to meet you."

Johanna smirks and shakes her head. "She loves to party. Please, do come in." Johanna opens the door further for Needles and me, and we both funnel into the apartment. "You're more than welcome to sleep in Astrid's bed. She won't be back until tomorrow afternoon, more than likely."

"Cool. I'm beat. Which one's hers?" Needles asks.

Johanna points to the bedroom on the left side of the kitchen while I drop my duffle bag by the door and look at her. She smirks slightly and her eyes rake over my body. I haven't had a sip of alcohol and I don't smell it on her breath. There's nothin' stoppin' me from sinkin' my dick into her. She's as good as any other woman, and fuck, she's attractive.

Johanna walks up to me slowly and as soon as she's within reach, I grab her by the throat, force her down onto her knees, and my cock pulsates in excitement. She fumbles with my belt, unbuckles me, and pulls my cock out. It stands at attention for her, needing some tension to be relieved.

Johanna licks her lips slowly and peers up at me through thick lashes. Her makeup looks impeccable, like one of those chicks where you know she took a long time to look this nice. By the time I'm done with her, I want her mascara to be running down her fuckin' face.

I dip my fingers into her mouth and pull her open for me. I'm not wasting my time here. I want her and I want her for one fuckin' thing.

My balls tighten while I rock my dick into her hot, wet mouth. She rubs her tongue against the bottom of my shaft, and I claim her mouth like it's her slutty pussy. I have both hands on her head at this point and fuck her like she's a whore I'm paying for. She gags around my cock, but I don't stop. The way she struggles only makes me want her more. It makes me want to bust a nut down her throat.

I shut my eyes and envision her soft brunette hair,

but hers isn't what I see. Instead, chocolate brown locks fill my vision and the same dark eyes to match it.

I'm not seeing Johanna. Instead, I see a ghost from my past. One that's very recently begun to haunt me again.

MARISOLE

While Bull drives, my heart pounds in my chest, unable to stop as my worries flood through me. I wrap my arms around myself in an attempt to keep my shit together. Chills run up my spine and Bull clears his throat once we're out on Route 1.

"My ol' lady was captive for a while, so, I think I know a little about what's goin' through your mind right now. Just know you're safe. No one is gonna hurt you."

Rosa offers me a half-smile and grabs onto my hand, giving me an encouraging squeeze. "Bull's right. You're going to be okay. You won't ever have to live life like you were. I promise this is over."

Immediately, I shake my head. "No, it's not. He's

my husband. He won't give up. Scar isn't the type of man who will let someone take what he believes is his."

Rosa's worry-filled expression turns into tight-lipped determination. "If he even tries to do anything, he'll be killed on the spot. This is something I can promise. You're my sister, Marisole. No one is going to fuck with you. If they even try, they'll have the Reapers Rejects on their tail."

"Alright," I murmur, not truly believing what she's saying.

"Sweetheart, why don't you take a breath and shut your eyes. I'm sure you're exhausted. We'll be to our destination in about twenty," Bull speaks up, and I nod, close my eyes and only focus on the movement of the truck. It's all I can bear right now.

I open my eyes after a while as Bull's making a right and we head down a road that looks like it's in the middle of nowhere. I keep my eyes open and look through the windshield. We come to a crossroad area where there're a few buildings on each side, almost like a small town. It's the kind that's gone in the blink of an eye. Bull continues driving forward and we must go straight for five or six miles. The next thing I know, I see a massive farm on the right. There are quite a few structures. A farmhouse, a couple of cottages, another small house, and then I spot a medium-sized house in the back near the barn. There are multiple silos on each side of the barn and Bull makes a right into the lane.

I make sure I'm looking around everywhere, needing to know my surroundings in case I need to get out of here. I know Rosa said I'm safe . . . but it'll take me a long time to believe it. As I look out Bull's window, the sun glimmers against the ocean. Holy hell, we're so close to the water. "Where are we?" I somehow muster up the courage to ask them.

"We're in Kitts Hummock," Rosa tells me. "Our friends have a club here, so we'll stay here for a bit and get settled."

Immediately, my neck tenses up at hearing this news. "Why are we staying here? It's too risky. Scar will find me." My worries slip past my lips and I realize I'm holding myself tighter than I was a few moments ago. I drop my arms and set my hands in my lap.

"I know you're worried, but this is for the best. I'm sure you need to rest after everything you've been through and—"

"No, what I need is to get out of here. Scar is going to come for me, Rosa. You don't know him. You don't understand what he's capable of." My voice is laced with fear. Normally, I'd keep it at bay, but I don't believe with my sister I need to. I have no problem showing her how terrified I am, and I have every right to be.

Rosa scoffs, appearing to be completely unimpressed. "I've dealt with men worse than that piece of shit back there. I hope you believe me when I say you are safe. You don't need to worry anymore, not at all. Okay? Just . . . just trust me," Rosa pleads with me, her eyes showing every bit of sincerity she has.

Sucking in a deep breath, I nod, and Bull pulls his truck next to one of the buildings and throws the truck into park. He unbuckles his seatbelt and looks right at me. "Rosa, how about you go out and let Gamble know we're here? I'm sure she's gonna wanna hear a rundown of what happened anyway."

"Yeah, you're right. Let me just help Marisole get out first and then I'll go find Gamble," Rosa replies.

"Go on ahead, I'm good." Bull waves her off, and Rosa ends up unbuckling her seatbelt and hops out the passenger side door. Bull gets out his side, slams the door, and walks around the front of the truck. He leans up against the door Rosa left open.

"She's not tryin' to suffocate you. I hope you know that."

"I do. She's only trying to help," I murmur lowly.

Bull shoots me a half-smile and nods. "Yeah, she rallied as many as she could to come down here and help you get out of that hell. Rosa's shit when it comes to admittin' her feelings, but fuck, she loves you. You're lucky to be related to someone as headstrong as she is."

"I know it. I'm grateful to have her in my life, but Bull." I stop speaking while I try to find the right words. Looking into his dark eyes, I say exactly what I'm thinking. "He'll stop at nothing. Scar will find me and he'll kill people to get to me."

Bull inhales deeply through his nose. "Sweetheart, I heard what he said to you. He called you an addict and I'll be straight up with you. The bastard doesn't give a flying fuck about you."

Unable to help myself, I scoff, "It's all a front. He's done this before, where he acts like he doesn't care about something. He does it to throw people off his game. Scar is possessive, Bull. He doesn't give up on anything."

Bull chuckles and raises his brows. "Trust me when I say he will, or he'll be six feet under. We don't play around with this kinda shit, sweetheart. You feelin' up to meetin' everyone?"

It doesn't matter if I'm feeling up to it. I need to do it regardless. I unbuckle myself and scoot to the side, put my legs over the seat and jump to the gravel. I weave a little to the left and right, and Bull puts an arm around me to steady me. Nervousness swarms over me and I breathe in and out slowly.

"Alexa, my ol' lady, when I pulled her out of the hellhole she was in, she acted like you are now. Take it a day at a time. I know you're gonna feel a lotta pressure to be normal, or like you're fucked up or some shit, but know you aren't. You have been through some shit and it's alright to give yourself some time."

I don't know this man at all, but I'm so grateful he's the one here with me. It helps that his ol' lady has been through something similar. He's not only being kind but patient as well. "Thank you, Bull."

Bull and I make our way to the clubhouse and he pulls the door open. I walk out of his grasp, knowing I can do this myself and I'm in awe. Is this what a clubhouse is supposed to look like? I'm used to torn up flags, chairs that wobble, and tables that have chips out of them from when fights break out.

The living area is massive, with nice leather couches. The type that has the buttons in them. I think they're called pleated? There are area rugs, a massive bar with ten stools and a built-in tap. Behind it is a state-of-the-art fridge, the type that tells you the temperature. Lord. Pictures hang on the wall of women in silhouettes. They're obviously nudes, but they look classy as hell.

"Everything alright?" a blonde woman comes up to me and asks. Her hair stops around her shoulders and there's a slight wave to it. She's wearing a cut, so I figure she's one of the ol' ladies, but as she grows closer, I see her patch that visibly reads she's the Prez.

No fucking way. A woman Prez? What planet am I living on?

"Yeah, sorry, just . . . taking all of this in," I murmur lowly, not liking all the attention on me. I can feel the eyes of the other guys in here staring me down. I'm sure they don't trust me at all. I can't even blame them. If they know where I came from, then they probably think I'm a spy or something.

"I'm Gamble and take your time. I actually have a room set up for you at the house across the lane. It's on the first floor, and there are rooms for the rest of your sister's club too. I'm sure it's been a crazy day, so how about we get some food in your stomach and you go rest?" Her eyes sparkle with sincerity, and I give her a nod.

Bull walks with me as I go forward, and Gamble leads me to a kitchen where she pulls out a prepared meal from the fridge and pops it in the microwave. "I'm so glad Rosa was able to get you out, Marisole. All of the madness is over with now."

I'm sure Gamble believes what she's saying, though I seriously doubt it. If you ask me, the madness is just beginning.

CHAPTER TWELVE

RAVAGE

"Fuck, I'm glad we're back," Needles comments as he gets out of the truck. I hop out myself and grab my duffle bag, glad this job is finally done. We made Konstantin beg for his fucking life and even then, we didn't let him live. After what he did, he deserved every bit of pain he got.

I throw my duffle over my shoulder and walk to the clubhouse, dropping the duffle bag in front of the door as I walk inside. A few of my brothers are here, but I spot Zane, Axel, Bull, Doom, Grim, and Zorro. "Hey, brothers."

"Hey, man." Zane rises and pulls me in for a hug. "How you doing?"

"Not bad, not bad. Good to see you."

"Likewise," Zane comments.

Gamble comes over to me and pulls me into a hug. "Thank you." And the moment she sees Needles come in, she unwraps her arms from around me and hugs him. "Thank you both so much."

"You'd better watch out. I gotta jealous ol' lady," Needles cackles, and Gamble smiles brightly as she pulls away.

"Somethin' happen?" Zane questions with a cocked brow.

"Needles and Ravage just got back from the Ukraine. They just dealt with Konstantin. He's the one who shot Ace."

Zane's jaw clenches and he nods. "Good. 'Bout time the fucker suffered." Zane's a father too, so I'm sure he can empathize with how Gamble's felt all this time.

"Don't ya think we should toast to this shit?" Zorro asks, making sure his gaze hits everyone.

Gamble smiles. "You know what, I think Z's right."

She heads over to the bar and Jugs is behind it, filling up shot glasses with vodka. Within a few minutes, everyone has a shot in their hand and they're all lookin' to Gamble. "To evening the scales, and never letting anyone fuck with us, or our loved ones."

We all down the shots and vodka burns the inside of my throat. I set the empty glass on the bar and make my way to the clubhouse doors. I really wanna get my shit back into my room and take a few minutes to chill. I don't say a word to anyone, walk out of the club, grab my duffle bag and cross the gravel lane until I'm at the house. I go in the side door, walk forward and make a right. I'm the last door on the left, so I go to the end of the hallway.

The door across from me is open and chocolate bronze hair catches my attention. Who is this? She turns, and my heart practically falls out of my asshole. I drop my bag in utter shock at who's standing before me.

"R . . . Ravage?" Marisole says my name in a breathless whisper, about as shocked as I am.

God, she's all skin and bones. Starin' at her like this causes me to be worried. What's wrong with her? Is she sick? I scan my eyes over her body until I see the bruises and sores on her arms, wrists, hands . . . and it hits me. She's an addict.

She shakes her head and backs up closer to the bed. "You can't be real. You aren't here. I'm hallucinating. I have to be." Her voice cracks with every word and emotion takes over her before I know it.

What the fuck do I do? Do I console her? Do I leave her alone?

Marisole drags her fingernails along her arms and scratches. She doesn't want to keep her eyes on me and looks all over the room. Dark circles are under her eyes, and I can see every bit of her collarbone. God, what happened to her? I haven't seen her in years ... not since I left her in Mexico. She ripped my heart straight out of my chest and broke up with me the night I proposed.

I take a step closer to her, and she backs away like I'm some demon she's trying to get away from. "Marisole," I say her name soothingly, hoping she'll let me come closer.

"N-no. You're *not* real. You're in my head. You can't be real." Her last few words come out in a cry.

"I'm real. I'm right fuckin' here. Look at me, Mari." I call her by the nickname I gave her back when we were dating and her eyes widen. She's terrified. Her hands are shaking and her lips are trembling, but she quickly starts scratching herself like there are fire ants crawling over every inch of her skin.

It doesn't take a genius to figure out what's wrong. "How long have you been using?"

Marisole's eyes lock onto mine and she deflects, "It doesn't matter. I need a hit. I'm going through withdrawal and I need a hit of something." Her eyes hit the floor, and I watch as the lightbulb goes off in her head. She walks right over to me with hope in her eyes. "Y-you can get it for me, Ravage."

"Why would I do that? You haven't answered my

question." She's desperate to get high, craving the one thing that numbs it all.

"If you get me the drugs, I'll tell you anything you want. I promise. I just . . . I need it, Ravage. I need it so bad." Tears form behind her eyes and for a split second, I feel sorry for her. I don't support this shit. Drugs only take you to one place—the ground.

Marisole's hope-filled eyes turn dark and angry. She tears herself away from me and pulls her arms close to her body. She mutters to herself, "I'll get some. I can get some for myself."

Marisole's a woman on a mission and walks past me, heads down the hallway, and I do something I don't think I'd ever do. "Wait. I'll get it. I just . . . I need you to wait on me. I'll get you some but give me some time." The last thing I want is for her to get something off the street, it could be laced with fentanyl and she could overdose. I don't want that for her. I know it's been years since we've last seen each other, but I've never stopped caring about this woman.

She narrows her eyes and looks nervous as hell like she's paranoid I'm gonna do somethin'.

"Come here. Sit in my room." I wave for her to follow me and she does, but she's not walkin' in a straight line and she keeps lookin' over her shoulder. Once we're in my bedroom, I pull the top drawer of my dresser open and grab a vape pen and hand it over.

"What is this?" She looks down at the purple and black pen.

"Weed."

"I don't need weed. I need some dope," Marisole grits with hunger in her eyes.

"I know you do. It'll take me a little bit of time to get you some, so, in the meantime, you stay here and smoke. It'll take the edge off for now. Trust me."

Marisole looks like she's debating what I've said, but she backs up to the bed and sits down. She brings the pen to her lips and inhales deeply, so I head to the entrance of my room. "I'll be back in an hour. Just stay here." Without waiting for her response, I leave, walking faster than I normally do. I need to get this shit for her and I know a guy. I mean, he sells dope, so he's not a great person, but I bet it's clean. He sells to lawyers, businessmen, and the uppity types. All I have to do is get there and hope she stays in my room until I get back.

CHAPTER THIRTEEN

MARISOLE

Ravage came back about twenty minutes ago, and I just finished cooling my dope down. I'm using one of his belts as a tourniquet for my arm, but I'm having a bitch of a time finding a vein. I slap my forearm, hand, and my mid-arm, but not one vein pops. "Motherfuck-er," I hiss as I bite down on the belt.

Ravage has shut his bedroom door and he leans against it, eyes focused on me as he watches from the other side of the room.

I yank on the belt tighter and pray a vein will pop. Scanning over my arm and hand for anything, all I see is marks and bruises. Nothing is popping. Dammit. I kick off my shoes and release the belt from around my arm. Now I wrap it around my mid-leg and I use my teeth again to pull it tight. A light blue vein pops on the center of my foot and I smile, knowing I can take this pain away.

I grab the bottle of alcohol Ravage brought me and use a cotton ball to clean my foot and wave air against my skin. I carefully inch the needle forward and a slight pinch ripples through my foot. I pull the plunger back as soon as I think I'm where I need to be and sure enough, blood shows up. I push the plunger down and pull the needle out just as euphoria floods through every part of my body.

I'm no longer nervous. Anxiety doesn't cast a depressive cloud over my body. Nothing matters anymore and I feel nothing except contentment. Breathing in and out through my nose, I shut my eyes and lean back against Ravage's bed. The drug spreads through my veins.

When Scar forced me to do this, it quickly became a habit. Now I use it as a way to cope with life. I'm just an addict now. Without heroin, I feel disgusting. My body doesn't know how to operate without the drug. Whenever I start coming down and going through withdrawal, sweats break out over my body, and soon after, it's like ants are crawling all over me. Disgusting isn't even the proper word for how it makes me feel.

I lay here for a few moments in the silence and after a bit, I scoot up. Ravage is still leaning against the wall and his eyes are locked onto my body. "Come on, you can't tell me you haven't seen other women shoot up."

He scoffs and shakes his head. "You're not wrong, but none of them are you. It's different."

It can't be different. We haven't seen each other in almost ten years. "Spare me the bullshit. We haven't seen each other in years. And in case you're wondering, I just use to help me deal with Scar."

An even more serious look crosses his face. "You mean you *used*. You're not gonna do it anymore, Mari. I can understand using to deal with shit when you're in a bad situation, but you aren't anymore. You're out and there aren't any more excuses, so enjoy the way you feel right now."

I laugh, the type of laugh that rolls through my entire body. "You can't be serious."

"Do I look like I'm fuckin' around with you?" he hisses from across the room. Kicking himself off the door, he comes toward his bed and glares at me. "Do you really think I wanna watch you OD like I have with many others? The answer is no. Hell, I can't believe you turned out like this, like . . ." He stops speaking completely and a disappointed expression crosses his face.

Now I'm the one scoffing. I lick my bottom lip and nod. "Yeah, hard to see me like this, isn't it? I'll break it down for you. Not everything is picture fucking perfect. Life is hard. I needed the dope, and I would've killed myself without it. Hell, I—" I stop speaking, knowing I don't need to tell Ravage shit. He isn't owed any answers.

"With your daddy, I'm surprised you even touched the shit."

I shut my eyes for a moment and take a few breaths, trying my hardest not to lose my shit. I don't want to, but I can't help it. When it comes to my father, I get so angry. If I'd just stuck up for myself as a young woman, I might've never ended up here . . . but look where I am now. God, this is laughable.

"My father wasn't the man you thought he was. He wasn't even the man I thought he was," I grumble, not able to look at my ex. The only person who will ever understand the disappointment I have is Rosa. Well, Rosa and our half-brother, Ricardo, but I don't even know where he is. Neither does she or Xavier. We barely know anything about him, so finding him is like searching for a needle in a haystack, from what Rosa's told me.

"Didn't take a genius to figure that out," Ravage tells me in an annoyed tone. It's like my mere presence is too much for him. Funny, considering a few minutes ago, he was so dead set on 'helping' me.

A knock comes to Ravage's door and he opens the door. "Can I help you?" He seems confused.

"Hey, have you seen my—" Rosa doesn't finish asking her question before she's in his bedroom and sees me sitting on his comforter. "Did you get high? How the fuck did you even get any . . . fuck, Marisole!"

"I was going through withdrawal, so I dealt with it," I mutter, not looking into her eyes.

"Are you fucking kidding me? You need to get clean, not get high. You . . . I . . . you don't have any reason to be using anymore. You're not with Scar. You're not being . . . fuck. You have a life, Marisole. You have a life now!"

I laugh at her innocence. She doesn't realize the type of man my husband is. "Rosa, I don't have a life. He will come for me until he has me again, or I'm dead. You're seriously underestimating him."

Rosa's upper lip curls in aggravation. "I've told you this already, but I'll say it until you understand, okay? He won't get within an arm's reach of you. Fuck, he won't even look at you without getting a piece of fucking lead between his eyes. I'm not fucking around here, Marisole. You're my sister and I'm trying so hard to make sure we don't lose each other. We've lost enough already, haven't we?"

"Yes, but you don't know him, Rosa. You don't

understand what he's like. He's possessive. He's crazy. He's . . . he's dark, okay? He won't—"

"He won't fucking touch you, Mari." Ravage looks right at me as he calls me by my nickname and Rosa furrows her brows. The way she's staring at Ravage tells me she knows we must know each other, but I doubt she has the details.

Rosa clears her throat. "You're not living your life in fear anymore. You'll get clean, Marisole. I have faith in you. We . . . we're not weak women, and I know you can do this." Rosa gets closer to the door and stops as she's in the frame. "Ravage, do you mind stepping out for a minute? I think we should have a chat."

Ravage nods and follows her. "Sure."

The door closes and I fall back on the bed, praying the euphoria lasts for longer than I expect. I don't want the pain to come crashing in like a wrecking ball. The dope . . . it makes everything better. It takes away all the pain and I know it's selfish for me to keep shooting up, but I don't think it's wrong to want a life without pain. I've just never known it without heroin.

CHAPTER FOURTEEN

RAVAGE

I shut the door behind me, and Rosa starts to walk partway down the hallway. Eventually, she stops and turns around. There's a lost look in her eyes and I know she has questions. I would, too, if I was in her position. Hell, there's no way Marisole even knew I was here. If she did, she would've given her sister a heads up or somethin'.

"We were engaged, or almost engaged," I cut straight to the chase, lookin' in her eyes. "Nine years ago, your sister gutted me like a fish and broke up with me while we were on vacation in Mexico. The same fuckin' day I met your father." I smirk as I scoff. Nothin' about the memories are good, but damn, it's funny how life works out.

"You're kidding." Rosa's mouth drops in surprise.

"I wish I was. Small world though, right?"

She shakes her head and shrugs. "I guess so. I . . . I'm naturally going to assume you actually give a shit about my sister then."

Immediately, I nod. "Without a doubt."

Rosa nods in affirmation. "Good, 'cause I need help getting her clean and I'm hoping you can help me with that."

"I'll do what I can," says the man who got her the dope in the first place. God, I'm a fuckin' dick. I don't want her goin' cold turkey, though. She might've conned me into gettin' shit for her, but she needed somethin'. I've watched plenty of people go through withdrawal. Hell, Butcher used to be an addict and he relapsed one time. The bastard was damn sure to go cold turkey without hits every now and again. I'm surprised the old fuck survived it. This is different though, Butcher obviously isn't the first woman I ever loved. Seein' her like this, a damn bag of bones with track marks and bruises all over her, it guts me.

I watched Butcher go through everythin' he did, but he's a stubborn old brute. I don't think I saw him as desperate as others might be. Marisole, though, she's gonna be goin' through it hard. With as many bruises and track marks as she has on her body, she must've been takin' hits every few hours at least. If she wasn't, I'd be shocked.

"I . . . we have to leave to go back to Montana first thing in the morning, and I don't think she can make the trip in her current condition. Not to mention, we have our own crap going on in Billings. I . . ." Rosa stops speaking and looks right at me. "I'll keep it plain and simple. I can't be the person to stand by her side and get her through the next couple of weeks. But . . ."

"I can. Don't worry about it." No way in hell am I not gonna be here for Marisole. Rosa's tryin' to ask me for help and while she's doin' it ass-backward I'll be here for her sister.

"Are you sure? I mean, I don't want to be a bother, but I didn't know you had a history with her . . . I'm just . . . if I was the only person, I'd make it work."

"Look, I mean no disrespect here, but I might even know Marisole better than you do. I can help her through this. You head back to Montana tomorrow and I'll handle everything, and within a couple weeks, she'll be clean." At least I hope she will be. I'm not a fuckin' addiction counselor over here.

"Babe," Axel's voice rings down the hallway and he turns the corner, setting his eyes on his ol' lady and me. "Hey, man, 'sup?"

"Ravage used to date my sister." Rosa doesn't even let me get a word in before she tells Axel my business.

I'm sure she was gonna tell him anyway, but she's cutting straight to the good shit right now.

"You gotta be fuckin' with me, right?" Axel looks at Rosa and then over to me.

"Nope." I keep it plain and simple.

"Shit, well, damn. Babe, we're heading back out now. Inc just called Zane. Something's goin' on with Syd," Axel tells Rosa, and she instantly looks concerned.

"Is she okay?" she asks.

He shrugs his shoulders. "I don't have a clue, darlin', but we need to get goin' now. We're all ridin' out." If they're all ridin' out, it has to be serious. Sydney is Zane's adopted daughter.

"If you need us, give me a holler. Gamble and I will always lend support wherever it's needed," I declare.

The Reapers Rejects MC has always been a great ally and whatever they need, we'll be there. I know the same goes for us if the roles were reversed.

Axel nods his thanks. "Cool. So, what're we gonna do about your sister? She good to travel?"

Rosa shakes her head. "No, Ravage is going to help us out for a couple weeks. Minus the issue back home, you know it's not like I have the time to dedicate at this second. I have that project with Octavia coming up for Vixens and we can't delay it."

Axel seems to be understanding everything his ol'

lady is saying, and it's all a foreign language to me. "Are we gonna come back and get her in a couple weeks?"

"Yeah, if that's okay?" Rosa looks at me, and I nod.

"Sure, it's no problem." It is a problem. Since I saw her on the beach, I prayed it was her, but now I know. It was Marisole and I don't want her to walk out of my life ever again. Fuck, I won't give her a choice. She left me once and people like us, we don't get second chances. I'm not gonna let this opportunity pass me up.

"Cool. I'll let Zane know what's goin' on. Will you be ready to bounce in fifteen?" Axel asks.

Rosa sucks in a deep breath and nods. "Sure. Just let me say goodbye to my sister."

Axel walks off and goes back the way he came in. The moment we both hear the door shut, we're walkin' back to my bedroom. Rosa surprises me, though, grabs my hand and looks into my eyes. She's nervous, terrified, the stress is showin' on her face. But what is she so afraid of?

"You have no idea how much I appreciate you doing this. I know it won't be easy. She's not going to be able to sleep. She'll be restless and agitated. That'll only be the beginning of her problems."

"I know. I've been through this before," I tell her.

"Oh, I didn't realize you used in the past."

"No, no. I mean, I've helped a friend through this. Her body will feel like it's on fire. She'll probably vomit, sweat a bit. Whatever it is, I'll get her through it. I won't let anything happen to her."

Rosa smiles softly. "I honestly believe you and I can't say that to most people."

"Well, I'm glad you can today."

We walk up to my bedroom door and before we open it, Rosa looks right at me. "Marisole isn't the only one in our family who's had problems with addiction. I haven't told her yet, but one day I will . . . I just don't think now's the right time. She needs to focus on herself, not on my past."

I offer her a sympathetic smile and open the door for Rosa. She heads inside and walks up to the bed where her sister lays on my comforter. Marisole sits up and looks at Rosa and while their voices are too low for me to hear, the second Marisole's eyes shift over to mine, I know Rosa's told her I'm going to be her guard dog.

What she doesn't know is I won't ever be quittin' this job.

I'll protect her for the rest of my damn life, and that's a promise.

CHAPTER FIFTEEN

MARISOLE

Sweat beads across my forehead and my head pounds as if there are drummers inside my head. I want to scream, cry, and everything in between, but I know nothing will make this better. It's been nine hours since my last hit and Ravage hasn't helped me get another at all. I know he's helping me get clean but doesn't he realize he's making me suffer? That's what this is, suffering!

Nausea rolls through my gut and before I know it, I'm grabbing the wire trash can beside his bed. My stomach contents pour into the waste bin and I pray for this to all end. I can't get through this. I'm not strong enough. This is only the beginning and things will be getting so much worse.

"I can't do this," I moan. Sliding over the side of the bed, I wrap my arms around the trash can.

Ravage sits up and turns on the light, illuminating the room. "You can, and you will. You're stronger than you know, Mari. I promise."

Unable to keep myself from scoffing, I roll my eyes. "I'm tired of men and their empty promises."

"I'm not your father," he growls and sits down on the floor beside me. Meanwhile, the weight of his words slap me like a ton of bricks.

"How'd you even know I was talking about him?" I question, lifting my head up from the can I look at him.

"It doesn't take a genius to figure out who you were referring to. Given the conversations I've had with Rosa, it was easy."

God, my sister. The one who left me here with Ravage. The one who said we'd get through life together . . . she abandoned me here with him.

"I need another hit, Ravage. This is too much. It's too much at on—" I'm unable to finish as more bile comes up. At this point, my vomit is just old water and sports drinks.

"No, you don't," Ravage tells me, and if I had the energy, I would wrap my hands around his throat and choke him out.

"I hate you," I growl lowly while chills run down my spine. He either doesn't care about anything I'm going through, or he doesn't understand what it's like. Any decent human being would get me some dope right now, just to take the edge off. We could tamper me down little by little and I'd be able to get clean that way.

Ravage stands up and goes to his dresser. He grabs a shirt and throws it on and I spot the tattoos going down his arms. I didn't even realize he had tattoos, but maybe I wasn't paying enough attention.

On his right bicep, there's a partial portrait of some sort of warrior. He looks to be from either medieval or ancient times. His entire body is a piece of artwork. I look over every tattoo, from the warrior to the lion on his alternate forearm.

"You don't hate me. You hate what I'm doing. There's a difference, Mari. Only you don't realize I'm doing this to help you better your life." Ravage grabs his cut from the hook behind his bedroom door, slides it on and before I realize what's happening, he's gone.

Figures, he's leaving me the same way Rosa did. She told me she'd be here for me for whatever I needed and what a joke. She's not here at all. She left, left me with my ex, for that matter. I push the trash can away and grab onto the side of his bed to pull myself up. He has two doorways a few feet away from each other, so I head over to one and pull it open. Sure enough, there's a bathroom on the other side.

Walking over to the shower, I pull back the curtain and turn on the water. I make sure it's hot. I want to step into this and feel something. I want it to burn my skin.

The water hits against the base of the shower and I strip out of my clothes. I turn the water on at the sink for a second, but only enough for me to gather some in my mouth. I swish it around and spit it out, put my hands on both sides of the porcelain sink and look at my reflection.

I barely recognize the woman in the mirror. It's been ages since I've actually stared at my reflection. I don't want to look like this, like this thin, desperate woman who's a shell of the person she once was.

Taking one hand from the sink, I run it behind my neck and breathe in deeply, trying to calm my anxiety creeping up. It's been horrible for the last couple of hours. My heart's been beating fast and paranoia comes crashing in. I feel the need to constantly look over my shoulder and my mouth is dry like I haven't taken a drink in ages. I have, though. Ravage has a plastic cup of water right next to his bed.

Hell, he stayed on the alternate side of it, giving me some space. He doesn't have another place to sleep in here, and I wasn't going to make him sleep on the floor. At some point, I remember he got so close to me and I told him I didn't want him getting closer, so he backed off, respecting my decision.

There's a towel on a rack hanging over the toilet, so I grab it and place it on the sink. I should be able to reach it from the shower. I pull back the curtain slightly and step inside, immediately sitting down on the ground. The hot water hitting my back burns just the way I want, a harsh reminder I'm here. I'm living and I'm breathing.

Even so, dark thoughts fill my head and combined with my anxiety, I've never felt more alone. My sister left me here to ride out the cravings and Ravage liter-ally walked out. I know I don't have to do this. I could walk out of this shower, dry off, put on some of his clothes, and sneak out of here. I might even be able to find my way to the nearest town and come in contact with someone who has something. It might not be dope, but right now, I couldn't care less. Anything would make me feel better than I do right now, right?

My stomach continues to churn and I think I might vomit, but somehow, I don't. It's one of the worst side effects of withdrawal, if not the worst. I wrap my arms around myself and continue to sit here, internally telling myself I can do this.

I don't need anyone.

I can get through this, even if I think I can't.

Sucking in a deep breath, I speak out loud. "I'm stronger than I think."

RAVAGE

I'm trying my best to be a good man, hell, maybe even a halfway decent one. The only problem is I've never been one. No one would even believe the shit that goes on inside my head. I was an okay guy when I was with Marisole, but after she threw me out of her life, I became something else. It's only natural, I guess. The rug was pulled out from underneath me and I didn't know how to cope.

The only way I did was by goin' to the bar to get drunk. I'd get in a few bar fights and some dude who ran some underground fights saw me. He talked me into takin' part in a few and long story short, that's how I eventually got to be part of the biker lifestyle.

I'm walking across the lane, hopin' Gamble's in the

clubhouse, but it's late. She's probably in her house with Hart and Ace. Any sane man wouldn't leave an addict in his room with a way to get out. I already know she has more than one way to get out. She could climb out the window in my bathroom, or head straight out my door and walk out of the house where all the brothers in the club sleep.

Here I am hopin' she won't walk out, that she's smart enough to realize what we're doin' is only gonna help her in the end. I step up on the porch and place my hand on the door to the club, pushin' it open.

A few of the guys are still hangin' around, havin' a drink, or chattin' with the others. Butcher and Needles are even shootin' a round of pool right now. "You seen Gamble?" I question Butcher, and he nods to the back. Good. I need to talk with her before shit starts to get a bit more intense. Marisole is still comin' down from the high, she may think she's goin' through complete withdrawal already, but she isn't. That shit stays in your system for a couple days before it gets really bad and it's only been about twelve hours since her last hit.

I head through the club and walk down the hall-way. Passing the kitchen, I spot Jugs on her knees in front of Judge. She bobs her head back and forth while I continue headin' down the hall. I go to the second to last door on the right and knock.

"Come on in," Gamble calls from the other side.

I put my hand on the knob and push it open, walk inside, and shut the door behind me. She's sittin' at her desk, scannin' over some sort of red book. "What's that?" I've never seen this in my life.

"A register. I'm keepin' track of everythin' we're spending to keep up with the bar here at the compound, and the new stuff we're doin' up the road," she murmurs, lookin' over the document.

"New stuff?"

"Mhm," Gamble murmurs, and I take a seat in front of her. "I bought the piece of property down the road, the little abandoned strip mall sort of thing." It looks more like a rundown outlet, but okay.

"What're you plannin' to do with that?"

Gamble looks up at me and laughs. "What a question. I'm still figuring it out. I know I'll fix up the structure, get new blacktop down, fix the parking area, so it's up to par, but I don't know if I'm going to funnel more club cash into startin' other businesses or if I'll rent them out to locals. Renting could be good, easy income, but we could start somethin' else up and launder cash through the guise of a nail salon or something."

"You really think we have the sorta location where people will come to get their nails done?" I cock a brow, tryin' my best not to laugh at her.

She shrugs. "I don't know. Maybe a hair and nail

salon, like a small sort of spa set up. I'm only mulling over ideas, Ravage. Now I know you didn't come in here for no reason. What's up?"

I swallow hard and suck in a sharp breath. "Rosa's sister, the one she brought from the Beasts of Brutality's clubhouse," I pause, not sure how to break it down for my Prez.

"Yeah, what about her?" Gamble questions.

"She's my ex-girlfriend, on top of bein' addicted to dope and all that."

Gamble blinks a few times and I know she thinks I'm pullin' her fuckin' leg. "Well, I wasn't expecting you to say that."

"Yeah, and I'm sure you noticed how the Reapers Rejects all rolled outta here."

"I did," Gamble comments.

"Rosa asked me to watch Marisole, and I told her I would. She didn't give me much of a choice, but I'm not gonna let the woman hurt herself anymore. She's addicted to dope, obviously, but I know she used it to cope with her fuckin' life."

Gamble gives me a sympathetic smile. She knows all about being trapped in a life that she didn't want. "Poor woman."

I nod, agreeing with her. "I need to get her through this next week 'cause you know it's gonna be rough as hell for her."

"Understandable," Gamble replies. "Are you two together, or?"

"No. I'm helpin' her get clean. There's nothin' more to this than a man helpin' a woman he loves out."

Gamble blinks a few times and clears her throat. "A woman you love?"

"No, a woman I used to love. She needs a friend right now, Gamble."

"That isn't what you said." She smirks, teasing me.

"It's what I meant. I don't want you thinkin' I'm bein' a selfish bastard when I'm tryin' to make sure she doesn't get high. The first week is always the hardest and you know it."

"Yeah, I do. So, what's the story between you two anyway?" She crosses her arms and leans back in her office chair, not paying a lick of attention to the ledger in front of her.

"You really want me to dive into that shit?" She can't be serious. Then again, I've never been close to any women other than Gamble. Nothing outside the occasional fuck with one of the clubwhores.

"I am losing my VP for a week or so. Don't you think I deserve to know?" Gamble asks, cocking a brow. It's like she's asking me to say no and see where it gets me, but I won't fall into the trap.

"I'll sum it up for you. I dated her when we were kids, teenagers. When I was nineteen, we went to Mexico to meet her dad. I was going to propose on that trip and she broke up with me. I stormed off back to our room at the resort, packed my shit, and caught the first flight back to the States. I hadn't seen her again until . . ." I don't bother saying anymore. She can put the pieces together.

"Fuck, you haven't seen this chick in ten years, and the first time you do, she's trying to get clean?"

"Not really her, more like us makin' her, but yeah."

"Damn, that's some intense shit."

"You're tellin' me." I sigh and run a hand over my head.

"Take as much time as you need with her, but she was pulled from that club we've been seein' around, right?"

I nod. "Yeah, from what I know, she's married to the Prez. His name is Scar. I remember the name, so I thought about it long and hard. I remembered Scar was the dude who Rage would go around tellin' everyone was his protégé."

"Shit, the guy's bad news." Gamble's assumption is more of a declaration.

"You got that right."

"And she's married to him?" She uncrosses her arms and cocks a brow. I know all the things that could go wrong are running through her mind. How do I know it? 'Cause I already did the same thing.

"Yep," I murmur, waitin' for Gamble to say somethin' else.

"Well, I know this won't be somethin' easy we're gonna deal with, but she's important to you. Therefore, she's important to us."

"Thank you. I appreciate it," I state as I rise from the chair, but Gamble's concerned gaze is still locked on me.

"Ravage . . . I'm all for protecting who needs it, but are you sure she's not . . . are you sure she's not someone you're going to claim? If so, I'll go hard to keep her protected forever, but if not, she'll be safe as long as she's with us and then she's on her own."

My heart practically stops in my chest. "Gamble, I'm not gonna make the same mistake again. She destroyed me and I'm not lookin' to get a repeat of the same feelin' ever again."

Gamble nods in understanding. "Okay, just wanted to make sure. I'll have church and explain to everyone why you're absent. You do what you need to and get her clean. Know you're in my thoughts, and so is she. The next few days aren't going to be easy for either of you."

"Thank you. I appreciate this more than you know," I tell Gamble while I walk to her office door, open it and leave. I make sure to shut the door behind me and make my way out of the clubhouse. Once the air hits my face, I let out a pent-up breath.

I told Gamble I won't make the same mistake again, but I don't know if I have that much control. The only thing I wanna do is wrap my arms around Marisole and tell her everything will be okay, even if I'm unsure of the outcome.

I lost her once, and fuck, but I don't wanna lose her again. This is another chance to make things right and her droppin' in like this. Fuck, it's like hangin' a hot dog in front of a Doberman on a treadmill.

MARISOLE

Three days. It's been three days since I took my last hit, and I'm on Ravage's bed, clutching his deep blue sheets under my hands. Sweat beads across my body and emotions filter through me like I'm someone who should be in a looney house. One minute I'm depressed, then I'm angry, and then I'm pissed. If the mood swings aren't enough, add in the fact I can't sleep, anything I eat comes up within a couple hours, and my gut's cramping like I'm having the worst period of my life. I'm just a bucket of joy over here, obviously. God, my sarcasm is ridiculous. It's the only way I'm coping with this all.

Ravage has since changed out the locks on his room and I can't get out through the door that leads into the hallway. He even added an outside lock on the window in the bathroom and I'm starting to feel like I'm a prisoner here. He's been with me pretty much twenty-four hours a day and left a little while ago. I didn't think he'd *actually* do it, lock the door and window, I mean. He kept commenting how he would if he had to leave but said the club knew he'd be sticking to his room for the next week or two.

I'm not an idiot. I know he's babysitting me like I'm a child. Hell, he wants me to get clean and while I understand why in some aspects but in others, I don't. He hasn't seen me in years and yet wants me to improve my life and make it better? Who is he to preach about what I should and shouldn't be doing?

My cramps intensify, feeling like someone has a knife in my gut and is slowly twisting it. I white-knuckle the comforter and groan out lowly, clenching my teeth as the pain surges through me. "Fuck, when will this end?" I practically cry to the ceiling and sure enough, tears start to leak from the corners of my eyes.

"Give it time. All pain ends at some point." Ravage's voice fills the room, and I shoot up, glaring at him while I now have my hands over my stomach.

"Where'd you find that saying, a fucking fortune cookie?" I snap and throw the most attitude I can in his direction.

He smirks for a second and shakes his head, holding a bag with the Devil's chicken and a cupholder with two large drinks. Chick-fil-A is my favorite . . . and the fact he remembered is astonishing.

"I'm hopin' your bitchy ass attitude is 'cause you're hungry as fuck, or should I say hangry?" He comes to the edge of his bed and pulls out a sandwich, large waffle fry, and a brownie, then hands me the soda.

As much as I'd love to take a bite into some of this food, I can't for two reasons. One being my stomach cramps. They're horrible, unlike anything I've ever experienced before, and two, I don't like his attitude. Not in the least bit. If it were up to me, I wouldn't be putting myself through this hell. Fuck, if I was, maybe I'd be tranquilized the entire time, so I don't feel everything if that's even possible in the first place. I don't know if it is, but I'm sure it would feel a lot better than this.

"I'm not hungry," I tell him straight up, knowing very well whatever I eat is going to come back up later.

He's on his way over to the chair in the corner of his room when he stops, turns to look at me, and gives me a glare that makes me think he's about to come over and slam me up against the wall. "You can't be serious, Marisole. When's the last time you ate, two days ago?"

I give him a curt nod. "Yeah, and I'm not going to eat. I'll just get sick again anyway."

I'm being honest, but my answer doesn't make him happy at all. "You'll eat 'cause I went out and bought it for you. Fuck, I had to drive a half an hour just to find one of those damn places. I didn't need to go anywhere after church. Hell, after church, where my entire club agreed to back me up and protect you from those bastards you came from."

I shake my head and scoot back on the bed until my back is hitting the wall. I pull my arms around my knees and stare right at him. "I didn't ask for you to do any of this." I'm so conflicted between being angry and grateful for what Ravage has done. Grateful I'm out of the Beasts of Brutality's grip but frustrated I'm in a new prison. I'm sure my sister never intended for it to feel this way, but it's what this is. How else would I describe it?

"You didn't have to," Ravage mutters, digging his hand into the bag. I pick up the red and white package the sandwich is in, take it from the packaging, and throw it right at his face.

"I never asked for this! I didn't ask to be locked up like some sort of prisoner. Don't you understand?! I didn't want this. I didn't want any of this. I didn't want to be here in Delaware. I didn't want to be with Scar, and I certainly didn't want to be with you!" I scream, tossing the soda at him too. The Styrofoam cracks against his chest and the drink covers his entire body.

His nostrils flare as he rises from the chair and, in record time, crosses the distance between us. "I don't recall askin' for permission, baby," Ravage hisses out every word, calling me by the pet name he gave me all those years ago. He proceeds to grab me by the shoulders and I run. My fight or flight instinct is activated and I use my legs to push me toward the door. I didn't hear him lock it, so maybe I can get out. Maybe I can be free. Only the second I have my hand on the doorknob, Ravage's weight collides on all sides of me. I hit the ground and his weight pressed up against me makes breathing seem harder to do.

It feels like my lungs aren't expanding at all and fear is the only thing I know. I hit the ground, desperately trying to breathe. Every time I try to take a breath, it sounds like an awful wheeze. The weight shifts from all sides of me and I'm forcefully pulled up. My shoulder blades hit the wall and his broad-shouldered body hovers over me. "It's okay. Whatever's going on in your head, don't listen to it. Everything is fine right now. It's okay." Ravage encases his arms around me and he holds me so tight, but the pressure around my body feels soothing in a way. "You're fine. Just breathe," he speaks to me in a low manner and sure enough, I can inhale lowly.

"I w-wish none of t-this ever h-happened," I sob breathlessly, tears streaming down my face. Ravage doesn't say a thing. He keeps his arms holding me close, and I blubber. "I was supposed to have a d-different life, and instead, this is h-how it turned out." I do my best to slow my breathing down as my thoughts come blabbering out. Going through with-drawal is hell but going through it with your ex, the one you have so many regrets about . . . it only makes everything worse.

"He told me I d-didn't have a c-choice and look where it l-landed us." Tears come crashing down and I can't hold them back. "I w-was supposed to be with you, n-not him."

CHAPTER EIGHTEEN

RAVAGE

It takes a couple of seconds for her words to sink in. Did she say what I think she just did? I keep my arms wrapped around her, but soon enough, wetness coats my t-shirt. I loosen my grip on Marisole, and she looks up at me with her big, red-rimmed eyes. "He told me I had to marry Scar. I wasn't given a choice, Ravage. I never wanted to hurt you and I know I did. I'm s-so sorry."

Shock. It's the only thing I feel. I should've known her father had something to do with the way we ended things, but what she said to me that day . . . it's like she had these pent-up feelings for ages.

"I'm sorry I lied to you. I'm so sorry, I can't imagine how . . . how everything felt."

"You lied to me," I state in a low tone as the reality of what happened starts to sink in.

She nods. "I thought I didn't have a choice. He told me if I didn't let you go, he'd get rid of you. I . . . I didn't understand *who* my father was back then, but somehow, I knew what he was capable of. I didn't want him to kill you, so I broke your heart."

"Fuck," I mutter in complete disbelief.

"I should've run away with you. I should've gone back to the hotel with you and caught the first flight out of Mexico, but I was a coward, a coward who wanted to appease her powerful father, and I've lived with regret ever since. I don't expect you to forgive me for it all, but I—"

"Marisole, shut up," I grumble, shutting my eyes. All of this pain. The way I pushed away anyone who got close over the years. It was all senseless. None of it makes any sense. None of it was justified. Marisole hurt me and I made sure no one ever got close enough to do the same thing again. I kept myself guarded, safe behind thick walls. Fuck, who am I kidding? I've barely been living.

He married his daughter off to Scar, but why? What for? Who is Scar to him?

"No, I can't. I've kept this shit inside for ages and now I need to get it out. He arranged for me to marry Scar since he was the protégé for one of his strongest allies. I was married to him, moved across the country with him until they settled here in Delaware."

I open my eyes again and her golden ones are locked onto mine. The guilt. The shame. All of it is vividly in front of me. "You got hooked on dope with them," I state, already knowing for a fact she did.

"Yeah. I . . . I think it was one of the only things that made me feel better." She keeps her eyes locked on mine and clears her throat before speaking up again. "He passed me around to his brothers, Ravage. Now, I'm not telling you this so you pity me, but I want you to understand what it was like there. I didn't shoot up because I'm an addict. I mean, I am now, but I . . . I did all of this to survive, and even the heroin wasn't enough. I tried to kill myself and they caught me before I was—"

"You did *what*?!" I grab onto the side of her face and neck, certain I won't be able to understand why a woman like her would wish for death.

Seriousness coats over the guilt in her eyes and she clears her throat again. "I was married off to Scar to solidify an alliance, not for love or anything like that. Then before I knew it, my father was dead."

I scoff, "The second your father died, the agreement he made was null and void. You should've left then."

She knows I'm right. "Things aren't so easy. If you

were me, you wouldn't have left either. Could you imagine what would've happened to me if I tried to leave? If he caught me trying to do it? I was happy when he caught me trying to kill myself. He just shot me up. I thought he was going to torture me!" she screams, pushing at my chest.

I'm trying so hard to sympathize with her situation. Marisole wasn't the person who made decisions here. It was her father. At the same time, it's not like she was powerless. She could've made different decisions and in doing so, it could've changed her entire life. Things might not have ended up the way they have.

"Marisole, what is going on in this head of yours?" I finally question her, and she jumps to her feet. I stand too and watch her as she paces the room—her face twists in aggravation and misunderstanding.

"Is he really dead, like are you certain of it?" Her question mind boggles me. There's no way I've heard her right.

Given I know who her father is, I can attest to it. "Why are you even asking me this right now?" There's gotta be a reason.

"A man like him," Marisole pauses, and I see she's struggling to find the words. "A man like him doesn't just die."

She takes a seat back down on my bed and I look

into her golden eyes. Marisole doesn't think her father's dead. It's obvious. But what does she think? Does she believe he faked his own death and Scar was somehow in on it? Does she think if she left, her father would come crashing in and put her in her place? Regardless, I won't let these ridiculous ideas plague her mind.

"Marisole, he's been dead for almost nine years."

We've been broken up for ten. Rafael would've died shortly after marrying his daughter off to a disgustin' creature of a man. I wonder if, as he rolls around in his grave, he regrets the choices he made. I wonder if he would've even cared.

Shaking my head, I suck in a deep breath and look at the food I had sitting next to my chair. "You haven't eaten, so get you some food. I'll be back later." I go to the door, walk out and lock it from the outside.

At least she won't be able to hurt herself.

RAVAGE

Thank fuck, I took all the weapons out of my bedroom. If I didn't, she might've already offed herself or attempted to, at least. Everything Marisole admitted to me a few minutes ago is still sinking in. Fuck, it might take a while for me to wrap my head around everything she admitted.

I head straight over to the clubhouse and walk right on in. Typically, I don't leave her alone since it's still early. She's on her third day through her withdrawal and the side effects from the toxins leavin' her body are comin' in hot right now. When I do leave, she's typically asleep.

Flora and Benita are sittin' on the couch, both women on one side of Needles. Fuck, he could be sleepin' with them both for all I know. Flora's his ol' lady, but he does shoot porn with her and they do group shoots when needed. "Flora, Benita," I call the women's names, and they both look at me.

"Yeah?" Flora comments with a bit of sass.

"I need you two to go sit outside of my bedroom. I don't want Marisole hurtin' herself."

Benita draws her brows together and looks at me like I've lost my damn mind. "Don't come at me with none of that talkin' back shit. You can do more than suck dick, so get your ass over there and do it."

Flora bursts out into laughter and Needles has a really hard time holdin' back his smirk. Benita, on the other hand, rises up from the couch and sashays her ass outta the club. Flora gets up and heads in the direction Benita went, but stops and looks right at me. "You know, Ravage, she's just pissed because it's the only thing she's *great* at." Flora giggles and walks to the door, leaving the clubhouse.

Needles now lets his laughter take over him, practically pissing himself. Sly walks in through the clubhouse doors and the second he sees me, he comes strutting up. "VP, I got some shit to fill you in on."

I turn my head over to him. "Yeah?"

"Mhm. I was just down in Rehoboth with Serpent like Gamble asked us. We've been followin' them Beasts of Brutality around and seein' what they're up to. Well, they were invited to a party. I overheard their Prez sayin' he was gonna go."

"When's the party?" I ask Sly.

"Tonight. Starts in an hour," Sly states.

Alright. "Needles, you in the mood to stir some shit up?" I glance back to my friend, who's already off the couch. He didn't even need a damn invitation.

"When have I ever turned down a good time?" He cackles, and Sly looks between us.

"You're comin' too, kid," I comment.

"Okay. I'll go fill Gamble in," Sly says, but I grab him by the back of his cut as he tries to walk in front of me.

"Nope, not today. I've got personal shit tied up with these fuckers and I don't need anyone screwin' with my plans," I tell him, and while Sly's eyes go wide and he nods, Needles hisses behind me.

I look over at Needles. "There a problem?"

"Nah, brother, but you're gonna be the one eatin' shit for this. Not me or him," Needles points out. If he's only concerned about getting in trouble, then I don't give a fuck.

"Rest assured, nothin' will be said to either of you. As a matter of fact, you two taggin' along isn't a request. It's an order. C'mon, I don't wanna be late to the party. It would be rude, wouldn't it?" I question, and Needles claps his hands together in happiness.

The three of us head out of the clubhouse and get on our bikes. Within a couple minutes, we have our helmets on and we're rollin' out of the lane, turnin' on the back road that leads for quite a few miles until we hit Route 1.

The entire ride, my hands bead with sweat and I find I'm clenching my jaw. When we're about to roll up to the bar the party's at, Sly motions with his hand for Needles and me to pull over. We do as he requests and all get off our bikes.

"I heard that dude tell his guys to watch out for the Knights and the Reapers Rejects," Sly tells me.

Good, the fuckin' idiot knows trouble is comin', and he's someone I have one hell of a bone to pick with. "Good, he knows we have a problem then," I grumble.

Sly leads us to the bar where the party is and instead of goin' in through the front, we all walk in through the side entrance. I head up to the bar, where I spot three cuts. One guy is on the side and two are side by side, but there's a bit of a gap between them. "We got your back, brother," Needles states while I walk up to the two standing next to each other. I grab them each by the back of the head and slam their faces down onto the bar.

The guy sittin' at the corner hops off his barstool, but Needles knocks him off his feet, quite literally, trippin' the big bastard. The two guys I just smashed against the bar whip around. One of them has a bloody nose while the other spits a tooth out in front of me.

"Who the fuck are you?" one grits out. He's about the same height as me and has blond hair. There's a rose tattoo on his neck and otherwise, he looks slow as fuck. I can take 'em. My eyes scan over his cut and I see his name—Scar.

This is the bastard who hurt Mari.

My nostrils flare and I have no control over what's happening. I throw fists and Sly keeps the other dude at bay. Scar and I throw punches left and right. He hits me and I hit him. At some point, he does an uppercut and lands a punch in my eye.

A gunshot goes off and everyone freezes. Naturally, I back up and check my body, lookin' for bullet holes. As I realize I'm good, I look at Sly and then Needles. They're both fine too. The person holdin' the gun is a short woman, maybe about five-foot-two with blonde curly hair.

"Get the fuck outta here before I call the cops and create a real issue. If you're not out within the next ten seconds, I'll make sure my next shot goes through one of you!"

Well, damn. A spitfire with a shotgun.

Scar waves and signals his guys to follow him

toward the front door while I motion for Needles and Sly to go out of the side door with me. We head down the stairwell and look around for the Beasts of Brutality, but I don't see them and I sure don't see their bikes.

Fuck. Where did they run off to?

CHAPTER TWENTY

MARISOLE

It's been three days since I've seen him, and now it's my sixth day since I've had any smack. I can't stop thinking about whether or not I did something to upset him or if he got mad about everything I said the other day. He hasn't been back since, so it might be true.

I've heard two women laughing outside my door off and on since I spoke to Ravage, and it's been quiet lately. They must have a key to the room 'cause I've been waking up to food on the inside of the room. I haven't heard the ladies today, so I stand up and walk over toward the door. Turning the light on, I find a bag on the ground and kneel to peek inside.

In the bag is a pair of dark jean shorts and a

Knights of Retribution t-shirt. Seems fitting given where I am. I take them out of the bag and continue looking through the bag. There's a can of dry shampoo and a brush, so immediately, I pop the cap off the can, shake it good a few times, and spray it over my head. I let it settle and pull the rest of the stuff out of the bag. There's a brand-new pair of size eight sneakers, a bra and underwear set, and an eight-pack of socks as well. I had a shower in the middle of the night to help me with the sweating. Sometimes it's awful and I need another shower. Then again, sometimes I take another shower to help with my gut. The cramping is sharp and even though it's the sixth day since I've had my last hit, it still feels like I'm being torn apart. I've always heard the seventh day is easier, but I have to make it there.

I think it's weird Ravage hasn't been here in a few days, given the fact he was here by my side through the worst of it. I'm still having a hard time swallowing that pill. After how I hurt him, he was still here and if that doesn't show what kind of man he is underneath his bad boy exterior, I don't know what does.

I take my time and change into the new clothes, kick off my old, nasty socks and put on the new ones and then take the sneakers out of the box. They're a cyan color, which is my favorite. Immediately I smile, figuring Ravage went and bought these for me. I can't wait to thank him.

It takes me about ten minutes to get changed and brush my hair. For some reason, I put my hand on the door and turn the knob. Surprisingly, it opens and I step out of the room. The hallway is well lit and empty, so I walk down and at the end of the hall, I make a left, heading past the stairwell and walk out the door. The gravel lane with white and cream-colored stone is a few feet in front of me.

Off to the right is the small cottage, then there's a bigger building in the center, and there are other buildings to the left, including a farmhouse with a wrap-around porch. I walk to the bigger building in front of me and as I grow closer, I round the corner and spot a man in a cut smoking a cigarette. "Mornin," the older man states. He's wearing sunglasses and has a salt and pepper tinted beard. Scanning over his cut, I spot his name 'Butcher'.

"Morning. You seen Ravage around?" I ask, keeping my voice low. I want to be hopeful this guy isn't bad, but I don't know him. The only bikers I've ever met have been foul men.

He nods and motions for me to follow him with his hand, so I follow closely behind him and walk inside the building. It's dark at first and then he flicks on the lights. The entire room is illuminated and I spot

Ravage with his arm under the back of his head, asleep on a couch. His left eye is black and blue, and he has bruises across his arms.

What happened to him? My stomach sinks and immediately, I'm walking over to him. I grab onto the forearm that's hanging off the side of the couch and before I can say a word, his eyes open and he's starin' right at me. "Guess Flora got the stuff in my room, huh?"

"Obviously," I murmur, staring at the rose tattoo on his left hand.

"You sound worried," Ravage has never had a problem speaking his mind, and he isn't wrong.

I glance up from looking at his hand. "Yeah, you look like shit."

"So did you when you got here." He cracks a smile, obviously fucking with me.

"Be serious for a second. I was worried when you didn't come back. I thought something happened to you."

He squeezes my hand, and I suck in a deep breath. "I did somethin' stupid and paid for it, so yeah, somethin' did, but it was my stupidity. I had a price to pay, so I paid up to the club."

I narrow my eyes. "What?"

"I blew our cover, what we were doin'. I acted out of anger and I should've waited . . . I was pissed about what happened to you and I acted a fool. That's the way to sum it up, but I'm good, just gonna be a bit sore."

"I don't like . . ." I stop speaking for a second while I try to gather my thoughts, but there's no other way to say this other than speaking my mind. "I don't like to see you this way. All bruised and hurt."

Ravage nods like he understands. "Now you know a fraction of what it was like when I saw you again. I don't think you realized it at the time, but you were hurtin', baby. You still are, but you're gettin' better every day."

He takes his hand from mine and rubs the side of my face, and for the first time since seeing him, I smile. Ravage smiles too. "I think you should have dinner with the club and me tonight if you're feelin' up to it."

An uneasy feeling floods over me. The experiences I've had with bikers haven't been great and the thought of eating dinner with a bunch of them? It terrifies me.

CHAPTER TWENTY-ONE

RAVAGE

Marisole and I stuck around the property for most of the day. I took her around the main area, we walked on the path Mammoth has been constructing for Riva. She complained how she didn't have a place to push Dahlia in the stroller, so he hopped to it per usual.

I haven't wanted to push her too far, so we've kept it leisurely. After a couple hours outside, I took her back to my bedroom and she ended up crashing on the bed halfway through a movie. We watched a comedy called *Bridesmaids*, which was the standard chick flick. When I realized she fell asleep, I turned the damn thing off and now it's a bit past five. Dinner's strictly at six every night, so I woke her up a few minutes ago and she's in the bathroom now.

I'm thinkin' about takin' her down to the beach beforehand. She hasn't told me much about what happened when she was with the Beasts of Brutality, but I'm not an idiot. She doesn't just have track marks all over her, but bruises too. I'm willin' to bet money her husband is the one who gave her the bruises. Maybe his boys did too. I don't know the circumstances, but one day I will get revenge for everything she went through. She shouldn't have had to, and I'm trying my best to keep a brave face on for her. Though, it's hard. Any time I get a free thought, the only thing I'm thinking about is blood. I want him to suffer for what he made her endure all these years. He treated her like a prisoner like she was a fuckin' slave.

I mean, fuck, I've heard the rumors about men who purchase women to treat them the way he did to Marisole. I'm not naïve. This world is dark, damaged, and I doubt it'll ever be good. People can hope for that type of shit, but the reality is it won't happen. People are selfish, too selfish to want to help others and let them have a good life.

Marisole walks out of my bathroom and has her hair in a high ponytail, but she has bangs . . . what the fuck?

"Do you like it?" She smiles brightly, walking toward me.

"I like you, period, bangs or not. But how the fuck did you do that?"

"I cut it, obviously." She rolls her eyes and laughs.

"Yeah, more like how did you?" I know I don't have scissors or a knife in here. The first day she was here, I made sure to take anything dangerous outside of the bedroom, and then when she told me she tried to kill herself, I made another scan. Hell, I took out belts, anythin' that could be dangerous.

"Trust me, you don't want to know," Marisole tells me. She should know me better than this, of course, I want to know.

"Mari," I say her name as a warning, deepening the tone of my voice.

"Fine. I found toenail clippers, so I used them to clip off my hair." At her admission, my face drops in disgust. I had a fungal infection on one of my toes not too long ago and she used the . . . God, never did I think some shit like this would happen. I have a hard time refraining from gagging and Marisole rolls her eyes and walks to the door. "Dinner's in a bit, yeah?"

"Yeah, let's go walk near the beach. It's been a while since I've been there and it's damn beautiful this time of day."

Marisole nods. "Okay, sure."

I walk over to where Marisole is by the door and we make our way into the hallway. Before I know it, we're walkin' down to the beach and I don't think I've seen her smile like this since she's been here. Her eyes are huge, like a kid in Disneyland.

"You good?"

Marisole turns to look at me and licks her bottom lip, "Yeah, it's just so beautiful."

At her comment, I furrow my brows. "You're actin' like you've never seen the beach before."

Her joy-filled expression drops from her face. "I haven't, at least, not in Delaware."

"What? You've been here for years and—"

Marisole immediately interrupts me, not letting me get another word in. "Ravage, he kept me at the club. I never left the property, not except that one time I did a deal for him."

Fuck. I don't know what I can even say to her right now. I don't think there are any words that could make things better, so I wrap my arm around her waist and walk with her. "I'm sorry for everything you've been through. You were dealt a shit hand."

"Yeah, but don't you think we both have? I mean, think about it . . . all these years apart and look where we are now."

"Still, if I knew where we would've ended up, damn, Mari. I would've fought harder, especially when I think about what you went through." I have no problem admitting where my heart is, and this will show me if the woman I've loved for as long as I can remember feels even a fraction of the same for me. I lied to Gamble about what I wanted with Marisole. I told her I'm just her friend, how I'm just helpin' her out, but it's all a lie. I'll never be able to be just friends with this woman.

Marisole inhales deeply and looks up at me. "This probably sounds crazy, but if I had to go through it all again, I would. I would as long as it led me straight back to you in the end."

Fuckin' hell.

"Keep sayin' shit like that, baby, and I'm gonna have to kiss you," I murmur, completely caught off guard by her words.

A flick of excitement crosses her eyes and she looks down at the ground before speaking. "Maybe I want you to."

Well, fuck. I'm not gonna keep holdin' myself back. Not anymore.

I use the arm I have wrapped around her waist and turn her against me. We're right at the edge of the beach where the water is merely a few inches from hittin' our feet. I take my alternate hand and cup the back of her head as I bring my lips down onto hers. This kiss is different than any other way I've claimed her mouth before.

I'm takin' my time with her, flutterin' my lips over

hers in a sensual manner. She moans against my mouth and my heart beats even faster, knowin' I'm givin' her exactly what she wants. I won't rush her. We'll take this slow and we'll continue to take it slow. Marisole has been through living hell and I don't want to be a dick when it comes to the way she might be feelin'.

I knew back then the same way I know right now. Marisole has always been the woman for me. Only, this time I won't let her go. I will never make the same mistake again.

CHAPTER TWENTY-TWO

MARISOLE

I've made it two entire weeks without taking another hit. I won't lie and say I haven't thought about it because I have, but the mental euphoria that takes over me is better than any drug. I spoke to Ravage about going to a couple of NA groups once things settle down, and he thinks it would be a great idea. I even spoke to Rosa last week and she's supportive of the idea too.

She asked me when I'm going to come to Montana, given I'm not going through withdrawals anymore and I broke the hard news to her. I'm not going to Montana. It made sense for me to go with her before because she's the only other part of my support system besides Ravage, but when she was making this plan, she didn't even know Ravage existed. Hell, I didn't even know being with him again would be a possibility, but here we are. He literally stood by me during the most difficult time. Sure, he wasn't around for three of the days I was going through withdrawals . . . but I needed that time alone. I didn't know it then, but it was important for me to take time and reflect. Plus, I wasn't the best person to be around anyway.

I'm still having issues with sleeping and my anxiety shoots through the roof sometimes. It can only be expected. I'm new at this whole recovery thing, but I truly intend to follow it through. I used heroin to cope with my life, but I don't need to cope anymore. I'm no longer a prisoner. I'm no longer being raped every day. I'm no longer being tossed around like I'm an object and not a person.

My life has completely changed in the shortest time. It's so short that sometimes I even have trouble accepting the fact this is real. I used to wake up every day to a nightmare, and now I wake up to a daydream.

I'm living in a place where I'm accepted, where people don't ask about my history. A couple of the porn stars give me dirty looks every once in a while, but I don't pay much mind to them. Flora, the woman who's Needles' ol' lady, tells me they're just jealous because I came back into Ravage's life in the blink of an eye. I didn't understand what she was saying at first, but she took the time to explain some women want to be with officers of the club. She's opening me up to a completely different type of biker lifestyle, but I'm grateful for the friend. Riva is super sweet too, but she mainly hangs around Gamble since she has a baby too.

I've been working on communicating more with Ravage, and for the last few days, he hasn't been around too much. He says there's a lot of club stuff going on and I don't pry. He did tell me the reason Gamble laid into him while I was going through withdrawal was because she had two guys in the club watching Scar. Apparently, they have someone they know from Baltimore working with Scar and they've kept a close eye on them. Gamble wants to know what they're doing working with each other. I can naturally assume it's bad, but I don't know shit.

Now I'm in Ravage's room, or rather, *our* room. I'm leaning up on the bed, reading a book Riva gave me. It's by Rae B. Lake and is called *Jameson*. I've been devouring it, and Riva wasn't wrong when she told me it's a great read, how it's action-packed and has steamy sex scenes. While I can't relate to Riva when it comes to having a baby, at least one common thing we can share is our love for reading. Scar never let me read, but Ravage is only encouraging me to get back into it.

He even got me a gift card to Amazon, so I can buy whatever I want.

The door opens to the bedroom and Ravage comes in. He takes off his cut and hangs it up behind the door, then peels off his shirt and starts to walk to the bathroom. As he walks, it's like he's doing it in slow motion. Every muscle on his upper half is tight as hell and glistens in the light. His dark eyes are focused and he's on a mission, but he comes to a stop and looks right at me.

"You alright?"

"You're *fine*," I say, not even realizing what I've said until he lets out a chuckle. He proceeds to toss his shirt in the hamper and comes up to me. He bends down, grabs onto the back of my neck, and brings his lips to mine.

I practically inhale the man, loving the way his lips mold to mine. He's perfect. Everything about him is perfect. Ravage pulls his lips from mine ever so slightly and smiles. "I know what you were doin'."

I bite my bottom lip, not hiding it at all.

"And we've had this conversation," he gently reminds me, pressing a kiss to my forehead.

He's concerned we'll go rushing into sex and it'll set me back, whether it's PTSD, flashbacks, anything. He wants me to get comfortable being with him before we take our relationship into more of a physical role.

On top of it, I need to go to the doctor. I haven't been to a gynecologist in ages. Riva got me set up with her doctor, so that's where I set up my appointment, but it's not for two weeks.

"I know you're getting antsy, but we just gotta wait. You just need to wait on me a little bit longer," Ravage murmurs, kissing my lips chastely. I lean into his kisses and whine as he pulls away.

I'll wait as long as I need to for him, but I really pray these next two weeks fly by. The fact he's being so patient with me and loving is . . . it's just another reason I've always loved him so much.

MARISOLE

4 Years Later . . .

"Ravage," I say my now husband's name and narrow my eyes on the tile options our contractor left for us in our unfinished kitchen. It's been a hell of a ride going with a stick-built construction, but at the end of the day, we'll have exactly what we both want. We're building it on the exact site Ravage walked with me when I started coming down from withdrawal. Geeze, how it's been four years already, I have no idea.

"Yeah, baby?" he answers, walking right up to me. I'm looking at two options. One is a metallic subway style, while the other is a traditional white. We're going with brushed nickel accents in here since I'm sticking to a sea green island color. I thought Ravage was going to kill me, but with the faux marble, it makes the kitchen pop with a beautiful brightness. Plus, it's my favorite color. Okay, so it's kind of a combination between cyan and sea green.

"Which one do you think we should pick? Angel wants a reply by tomorrow." I hand Ravage the two options, and immediately he picks the metal, which is a bit shocking.

"I'm gonna be stuck in this house with you and a carbon copy, so give me as much manly shit as I can get." Ravage chuckles, wrapping his arms around me to cradle the small bump that's finally decided to pop out. We just hit the five-month mark and were told it's a baby girl. I'm thrilled, more excited than I can ever say, but at the same time, I'm scared.

I never thought I'd be the motherly type, but here we are.

"Fine, fine," I laugh, leaning my head back against his shoulder.

He smiles widely and kisses my forehead. "I can't wait until we're outta that small ass room and in here. I wanna cuddle you on that couch I picked out, watch movies with you, see our lil' girl on the carpet with Petunia."

"God, she's going to love the baby." Petunia is our six-year-old rescue from the Brandywine SPCA. She's a blue and white pit bull and the sweetest thing. One thing that's been a huge part of my recovery is going on long walks. She's the perfect partner for me to have. Ravage calls it scary dog privileges, and I don't think he's wrong.

I know Scar is dead and he isn't ever coming back, but it doesn't mean he never had friends who would hunt us down and hurt us. Since I've been pregnant, my mind's been plagued with memories from the past, worried if someone's going to come out of the woodwork and haunt us. I truly hope not, but I do know I'm in the safest place I can be.

Petunia's in her crate in our room in the house by the club, but she's the perfect girl. Everyone at the clubhouse loves her too. When Ravage proposed to me, he had her bring me a box and drop it in my lap. I opened it up and found one hell of a sparkler. It was the sweetest, best way to be proposed to. Besides Ravage and my sister, Petunia is the thing I love the most in this world. She's truly a member of our family.

She was in our wedding too, and when it gets too cold here in the winter, I have sweaters I put her in. Mugshot and Needles love to pull my leg for being *that* type of dog mom, but I couldn't care less. At the end of the day, I know they'd be doing the same thing if Petunia was their pup.

"I can see it on your face. You're worrying," Ravage points out, walking in front of me.

"I wasn't, but now I am." We've had so many construction delays and I'm concerned we won't be settled before the baby comes.

"We're gonna be fine, and worst case, if she comes bustin' out the gate early, then we'll be in our room for a bit longer. It'll be snug, but we'll make it work. You trust me, don't you?" Ravage loves to ask me this question. It's a way he hides being worried too. Over the years, we've rediscovered each other and our quirks. For example, when I say I'm not hungry, it a hundred percent means I am, and if he doesn't bring me food, I will withhold sex from him until he brings me something super scrumptious. I usually make him drive out to Georgetown. There's this small bakery owned by two Hispanic women, but they make homemade empanadas. They're delicious, the best I've ever had. Needless to say, when he's in the doghouse really bad, he'll make a drive down to get me what I want.

Figuring there's no point in being too stressed, I simply nod and lean against him. If someone would've told me where he and I would've ended up, I would've laughed in their face and told them they were crazy. We had so much history and never in my wildest dreams did I think our lives would ever cross paths again, but I'm glad they did.

If push came to shove, I'd wait a million years for him because Ravage is the person I'm supposed to be with. While I'm scared to be a mother, I can't wait for the moment he sees our little girl because he'll be the best father in the entire world.

A lot of people say when you know, you know. We might've had to go through hell, but I'd do it all again to end up with him. He's undoubtedly the love of my life.

THE END … FOR NOW.

Hello Readers,

I hope you enjoyed reading this book as much as I loved writing it. In the beginning, it was really hard to write it, given what Marisole endured during her time with Scar. Although, as the story progressed, it became more about her recovery, overcoming her demons, and solidifying a life with Ravage.

The next book in the Knights of Retribution MC will be Mugshot's book, Bleed on Me. Keep an eye out for when it goes on pre-order. I already have the prologue written and it's going to be very enthralling. Scar will finally be getting what he deserves and Mugshot will be helping Ravage deliver the blows, quite literally.

As always, thank you for being on this ride with me. I can't wait to bring you Mugshot's book. Per the title, things will be very dark.

XOXO,
Elizabeth

Want to listen along to the songs that helped inspire
Wait on Me?

Listen Here

Pre-Order Sydney's Battle: